The
CABLE DENNING MYSTERY SERIES

by
James P. Alsphert

James P. Alsphert
presents

DEATH BECOMES YOU!

A
Cable Denning
Mystery

BOOK
12

Published 2018 by Movies of the Mind

Copyright © 2010 by James P. Alsphert

Printed in the United States of America

First printing, 2018

ISBN-13: 978-1-64056-020-8

MOVIES OF THE MIND
www.moviesofthemind.net

CONTENTS

Preface

The Creation of the Cable Denning Series

Death Becomes You was originally entitled *Murder Becomes You*. Actually I had no intention of writing more than this one 233-page book. Though I was always writing things from an early age, I never considered myself a *writer*! This book was meant to be a vehicle for a reminiscent look at my Dad's life and the people he knew, which would include Al Newley, my model for Cable Denning—who really did become a private detective after being a Los Angeles police officer. I've incorporated in these pages, recollections of my earlier life with a chain-smoking, alcoholic parent, who was a brilliant man early in his life but drank most of it away.

This first and singular Cable Denning book, *Death Becomes You,* takes place in 1942 as World War II began for us. It covers a year of turmoil politically, economically, socially and romantically for Cable. He was born in 1900 and thus is no young man star-struck with the world, but the book reveals the life style people lived and the atmosphere during that time in the United States and especially Los Angeles.

As I, myself, became fascinated with the character of Cable Denning, I felt a pull to write another book, *Kill Me in G-flat.* This one taking place in 1948. A publisher in New York asked what Cable Denning may have been like as a much younger man when he was first a police officer. The thought of that intrigued me and so I embarked on my adventure of writing the Cable Denning Mystery series in chronological order beginning with

Golden Throat (1927) where Cable is a 27 year old cop. He leaves the L.A. police force and becomes a private detective like his real life model Al Newley.

The first 2 books I wrote have now been inserted into the series as they occur chronologically...that is why this book is now shown as Book 12.

So as you read my first 'baby', I hope you enjoy it from the perspective of a brand new author writing a story resembling aspects of his own early life experiences and having that idea transform into a major murder mystery series.

JPA December 2014

Prologue
The Battle of L.A.

Sometimes late at night a lonely sax blows through my head and the footsteps of strangers passing by echo all the dreams that never came true. Memories flood in like pieces of lava falling out of the sky, burning a hole in your brain. It's like life gives you a bad rap and you never find that ringside seat, but the fight goes on with or without you. So you become a nonentity, a statistic at the end of the tax roll. And being nobody comes with a price—not just for me but for all the faces out there that I see silhouetted in the lighted windows of Clifton's Cafeteria, as I walk by. The sounds of the city are like a giant, roaring dragon that never sleeps. But for me they're like a dope addict's fix that reminds me that blood still flows through these ol' veins and that cigarettes, booze, and hot dames haven't killed me yet....so far. Still, there was always a feeling gnawing in my gut. The one that says sameness is a lethal disease and snapping photos of errant men and women caught up in the shadows of a moral trespass gets old after a while—and in the end, who really gives a damn? Same was true for the girl who worked in the cosmetic department of The Broadway at Hollywood and Vine, or the plumber who fixed the same sink or toilet but at different locations, or the streetcar conductor punching transfers to the same destination for the zillionth time. And...aaah yes...when the night breezes came in from the sea, I can smell caramel corn from the vendor down the street. The wonderful smells of those delicious corn tortillas and roasting jalapeños wafting over from Olvera Street or the sweet

1

scent of newly made chocolate from a nearby confectionary.

But most of all for me, it was the *music*—the high I got when I stepped down into the sights, sounds, and smells of *Mindy's*, *The Blue Gardenia*, or *The Neon Flamingo*...joints that were alive with people celebrating life, love, misery, a kiss in the dark, or a heartache that can't be numbed with an aspirin. So here they congregated, drawn together in a raucous collage of sound by a beautiful babe in a low cut red-sequined gown, warbling the great music of Kern, Porter, Gershwin, Mercer, or Berlin and played by real pros—musicians who came up the hard way, living like salamanders deep in a dark, wet cave somewhere—forgotten by the outside world. But the march of time was changing a lot of things. Lonely wives, girlfriends, and lovers sought out escape in the din of those noisy, dark cabarets and cheap gin mills when their fellows got shipped overseas or were killed in action. But that sexual body we carry around with us kept it's ache of desire like a pinball that, once shot out of the tube, has to go down from there, no matter how many bumpers or holes it hits on the way—or what the final score tallies at the end. The ball still ends up at the bottom of the machine called life. Women who would never have crossed that threshold into the world of temptation were drawn into those smoky dens of laughter and sultry music like moths to a flame to let down their hair, have a few laughs, and maybe even go home with someone because the loneliness was eating a hole through the moral fiber that kept them going to church on Sunday or kept alive the hope that Johnny would come marching home soon.

Yeah, this was my city and as stinkin' rotten as it was, its flip side was an organic magic that called to an empty place inside, lifting you an inch or two above the ground. The nightspot was an escape from the grinding everyday phoniness found in the trenches out there. A sanctuary carved out of the seedy guts of a growing skyscraper world. Somewhere to go on a restless night when every other part of your world added up to zero.

But this was 1942 when everything was changing. For one thing, we were at war with the empire of Japan whose planes had clobbered us but good last December the 7th in the Hawaiian Islands. But war, I figured, was always caused by people who would profit from it, via money, power, and/or a piece of the real estate. Maybe if humans weren't so perverse and stupid, there would be peace in the world. I don't know. Seems we walk around biased, fueled by prejudices and paste-on Sunday school smiles, pretending....always pretending that we know something, when really we know so little. I lived in the heart of Hollywood, where the thriving movie industry brought in millions of hapless souls weekly to peer at images on a silver screen, projected by a magic lantern, while countless young starlets fled to the day-couches of the movie moguls for their moment of glory on that screen. While downtown, deals were being made under the table to make sure the City remained in the hands of the rich and powerful, while the poor and disenfranchised eked out rent and food money—and maybe forty-cents extra for a Saturday matinee at the Strand.

Phantom Notes at The Neon Flamingo

The music ran through me like smoke rings hung on descending notes. The combo was playing Duke Ellington's *Solitude*, a place I dwelled in when I turned the key to my apartment at night, or picked up a woman's perfume taking me back to times with an old flame. Funny how songs evoke times and places, things you've experienced and memories—some happy, some painful. When I was 27, I fell in love with a beautiful doll whose name was Honey Combes. She later changed her name and became actress Lana Lorren—and died at 22 from a bullet hole in her heart because she was in the wrong place at the wrong time and loved the wrong guy.....me. Some things you bury so deep they can never be retrieved. Other songs take you away and project you into some fantasy dreamed up by the place in you that screams—the one that says your life is bleeding away and you need to come up for air. But music had magic. How else could waves of melody and harmony imported into your brain from a bunch of notes from a piano, bass and a muted trumpet turn you into jelly and tears?

I knew it was sometime after midnight. I sat at a favorite corner booth slugging down honeyed whiskey in a hot snifter and filling my ashtray with Lucky Strikes. I was looking for someone. I came down into this smoky pit of cheap gin, lost men and women and great music, because a certain party owed me some dough.

Then I saw her come in. She moved like a cat. Her black hair was slicked back, her eyes squinting as she adjusted to the semi-dark of *The Neon Flamingo*. Her body settled quietly as she slid into a booth at the opposite end of the room. She was wearing a beige wool suit with shiny black high heels and a single strand of pearls hung around her neck. I fortified myself with one more slug of whiskey. I walked over to her booth. "Well, hello...."

"Mr. Denning. My...what a pleasant surprise." Serena Garfield said. Her one claim to fame was that she was married for one night to a young actor named John Garfield, so she kept the name.

"Yeah...it's Miss Garfield isn't it? Fancy meetin' *you* here," I said, looking at the healthy cleft of bosom just under that pearl necklace. "So, have you been thinking about me?"

She winced slightly. Then she reached into her purse and drew out a wad of money big enough to support me for a year. "Yes, Mr. Denning, I have." She counted out a couple of hundred clams. "You more than earned it. You see, Harvey's infidelity reaped a hefty reward. Now I am an estranged wife with a pre-alimony settlement."

"Well, I'm...I'm glad it worked out for you." She handed me the money. "Thanks. I was wonderin' what happened. You know how people kinda disappear when it comes to dough..."

"Not me, Mr. Denning." She looked me over from head to toe. "I am now a free woman. I may go back to visit my folks in Greece soon, but in the meantime, I...I, uh, might enjoy the company of a gifted private investigator who takes great Kodak photos of overly passionate men in compromising positions."

"Yeah, I got lucky. Poor Harvey. Never knew what hit 'im, eh?"

"Oh, yes, he did, Mr. Denning. I hit him for about three hundred thousand dollars. But Harvey was never very exciting. I love a man who lives on the edge...." She licked her lips as the waiter delivered her drink. "Do you know any such man who lives on the edge?"

"The edge of what, Miss Garfield? Life comes with an assortment of edges."

"I always liked your patter. Now that we're no longer client and private investigator, may I call you Cable?"

"If you like." The combo started a lively version of Noel Coward's *Mad About the Boy* and she looked up at me with eyes that suddenly became very sentimental.

"Hear that music, Cable? Will you dance with me? I've always adored that song."

"Sure, why not, Miss..."

"Serena, please."

I took her hand and we went out onto the tiny dance floor. Only one other couple was dancing, but it looked to me more like a 3:00 a.m. clinch. She put her body close to mine and we moved around like we knew what we were doing. "*Lord knows I'm not a fool, girl, I really shouldn't care...Lord knows I'm not a schoolgirl, in the flurry of her first affair....* It was 1934 when I was young and beautiful," she was half-singing to me. "*This odd diversity of misery and joy...if I could employ a little magic that would finally destroy, this dream that pains me and enchains me...but I can't....*" We stopped dancing. She got up on her toes to kiss me. "*I can't...because I'm mad about the boy...*"

The music ended, the other couple left the floor but we stood there looking at each other. "You're pretty good with lyrics," I finally said.

"I'm pretty good at other things, too." She didn't have to say anymore. I took her back to her table. I paid the tab for both of us and we left. We walked out into the smell of restaurant garbage rotting around the alley. "Shall we have a nightcap at my place? I have a very nice view. One of the new sky-rise apartments on Wilshire." She took out her purse and scribbled an address. "Meet you there?"

I helped her into her car. "You know...I'd like to, Serena. It's not that you're not desirable, but I have a rule about good women who seem like easy dames and easy dames who really aren't good women. Call it a character test. What you did to Harvey, you'll do to the next man who gets caught in your venus flytrap. Naw... thanks anyway, but I think I'll pass on that nightcap. Thanks for the dance...and oh, the goodnight kiss. You might even have a fine singing voice beneath all that makeup."

She started her engine and screeched away in her maroon Cad. I patted the cash in my right pocket with my hand as a siren pierced the night and reminded me I was in that city that didn't sleep. I got into my little Dodge coupe and drove home.

The Winston Women

Sameness had a way of killing off the instincts that told you something was missing in your life. Once you lose caring much about yourself, the wheel starts turning in the other direction. You wake up one day with that empty bottle of gin next to your bed and an ashtray overflowing with cigarette butts. Then you take stock.

Suddenly you remember you're nobody, and outside of a few clients, the only person who says good morning is the mailman. At that moment as you stagger to the bathroom, you realize nobody cares about what you say, think, or do...as long as it doesn't get into *their* face. You throw yourself together, cut yourself shaving and wince from the sting of the septic stick. You manage to put on some decent clothes, but it's hot out, so no tie today. Just the white shirt and the dark jacket and pants with shiny shoes and socks that've seen better days.

The phone rings with an impatient wife at the other end, demanding that you catch her husband "with that hussy" or you don't get your fifty-bucks for two days' work. You stall her off, but you don't really care. He'll show up. And they'll either divorce or make up. It's always the same. I'd sunk to that—snapping Kodaks of cheating husbands as they're leaving strange addresses. Or better yet, a cheesy afternoon shot taken through a window, of the two of them rolling around in the sack— that can get you a few bucks more...in case it ends up in divorce court.

Then Fredericka Winston entered my life. She was a tall, winsome broad with glossy dark-red lips, blonde hair and blue eyes intense enough to sink a battleship. I figured her to be somewhere around 30, she had a slight British accent and told me a crazy story like a lot-ta dames do, most of 'em about men. And this was no exception. She wanted me to trace down some ex-lover of hers, and then when I found him, deliver an envelope to the mug. At least that was the way it was supposed to go.

8

Yes, the world was changing in 1942. Strange things kept happening that the newspapers and the radio glossed over like angel hair on a Christmas tree. Case in point: last month, February 24, 1942, the skies above L.A. and Santa Monica were invaded by aircraft of unknown origin. The Japs had clobbered the American forces at Pearl Harbor this last December 7th. It was assumed, then, that the strange 'invasion' of February 24th was their next step in an attempt to conquer America. At least that's what the press tried to frighten us into believing.

For several hours things went very strange...like someone was dreaming the Mad Hatter's tea party and you were forced to sit at the table. A total blackout was ordered. I remember glancing at my watch. At about 3:16 a.m., machine guns and anti-aircraft ground crews fired upon weird looking spacecraft in the skies above them, searchlights caught glimpses of nothing the army or navy had ever seen before. I was up pacing my office all night, listening to the thunder of the big guns and the sirens screaming. It went on sporadically until after 4 a.m.

At about 7:20 on the 25th an air-raid siren signaled the "all-clear", the blackout order was lifted and we went back to our normal dull lives. The droll Secretary of the Navy, Frank Knox, said on KFI the next day that...and I quote, "It was a false alarm. No detectable enemy aircraft were actually spotted and we fired upon several weather balloons we had launched to use as markers...." Well, I got the gist. They always lie when they don't know...*or* they know the truth and they're not tellin'. That's how governments pull the wool over the eyes of the poor dumbed-down public. Make it up, tinge it with a little fear and like a gambling casino, stack the deck to favor the house.

Ah… but this classy Miss Winston was the next client on my agenda. I had found her lover man, a guy named Leon Berguson. He was probably a no-account gigolo— the kind who preys on rich babes. Anyway, I had agreed to make that delivery the next day…Tuesday…at some house up on Lanterman Terrace in the Silver Lake area. When I got there, the door was open. I walked in and ended up on the floor. "Aaaagh", I groaned.

Chapter 1

THE MYSTERY OF
LANTERMAN TERRACE

My head felt like Boots Blake's ulcer after a seven-day bender. I rolled off the floor down a couple of stairs until I could grab the banister. Finally I sat up. It was all a blur. Was it Saturday or still Tuesday when I was supposed to meet that crazy dame at some...or...? I even forgot where I was. Some nervous canary kept flitting back and forth between my brain lobes. Funny how you can be okay one minute and knocked out silly the next. I always wondered what long-term damage my head might have sustained after fifteen years of flat footing as a private dick. At least my neck still had physical movement.

"Aaagh," I groaned again. In the semi-darkness I fumbled for a light switch. No luck. I made my way to a window, peaked out a curtain that had the smell of stale cigarette smoke soaked into it. The sun had already disappeared behind the distant sea and the afterglow looked like a cross between smog and pink salmon. Then suddenly I remembered. I was supposed to deliver an envelope to Berguson. Somebody had clubbed me from behind with a sap and I went down for the count. I felt inside the breast pocket of my rumpled coat. My wallet and money were still there. At least it wasn't robbery. Or was it? I fumbled around in my other pocket for the envelope I was supposed to deliver. It was gone. And whoever slugged me didn't want me to see his face.

And then I remembered. Thirteen days. She still owed me for thirteen days. Twenty-five bucks a day plus expenses, like gas and food. After all, Signal Oil was ripping the public off with that damn stuff as high as 22-cents a gallon! So she owed me. I had to get back to my place and glue myself back together. I thought that bottle of smooth gin would do fine just about now...all of it.

I left 2433 Lanterman Terrace. As I walked toward my little black coupe, my head pulsed with each footfall. I felt around on the back of my head and discovered my attacker must have been playing golf on it, 'cause he left his ball sticking out somewhere between my ears...and it hurt. I opened the glove compartment as I plumped down on the car seat. I found an un-opened pack of Lucky Strikes and boy did that little red logo in the cellophane look good! I dug a match out of my pocket and lit up. "Ahhhhh," I sighed. The smoke poured into my lungs like a welcomed soldier coming home from the war. I relaxed, still trying to put together the pieces. I drove off wanting to get something to eat, but that gin kept calling me louder.

By the time I climbed the stairs to the second floor of my office building, I had learned it *was* still Tuesday and I had probably been out on that floor for a couple of hours. I opened the door to my disheveled office like an alcoholic with one thought. I got to my desk, opened the lower left-hand drawer and found the bottle of gin. I poured abundantly into a dirty water glass I keep around, one of those handy items no bachelor pad is complete without. Then I made my way to the bathroom mirror and dared to take a look. Some of me had survived the blackjacking, but I suspected some of me hadn't. My head still hurt like hell and I had a nasty little cut on my upper lip, which explained the blood on my light-gray suit jacket.

Just as I finished cleaning up a little, the phone rang. It didn't ring a lot these days, so I was anxious to pick up the receiver and hoped it was a job.

"Yeah, hello...Cable Denning here...."

There was a long pause. Then a sultry, warm female voice heated up the wires between us as she spoke. "Yes...Mr. Denning, I need to see you right away. I'm Eleanor Winston—Fred's sister."

"Fred?"

"I'm sorry...Fredericka...my sister. I believe she recently hired you. You *are* the private detective, aren't you?"

"Yeah, I'll say, sister—she met me alright, at least her mug of a boyfriend sapped me with a good one over the noggin when I arrived at her joint on Lanterman Terrace earlier this afternoon ...."

There was another curious silence. "I'm sorry. Why would he have done that? Were you out of line with Fredericka?"

I had already had enough of the fuzzy dame at the other end of the line. "I don't know what you're sellin', lady, or what your crazy sister is up to. All I know is that I was hired to deliver an envelope to your sister's address..."

"But my sister doesn't live on Lanterman Terrace, Mr. Denning. There must have been some mistake. Did she tell you to meet her there—and did you see her when you went there?"

13

Now it was coming back to me in spades. Not only did I *not* see the lovely Fredericka when I went to the rendezvous, but the envelope I had arrived with was missing when I left. I explained this to the sultry-voiced woman at the other end of the phone. "Well, you see Miss Winston, it's like this...your sister came late last night as nervous as a clam on a hot griddle. She gave me the envelope. It had the Lanterman Terrace address on it. And oh, by the way, your sister still owes me for thirteen days of pounding the pavement to track down the whereabouts of one Mr. Leon Berguson, and now I assume, perhaps the contents of that envelope."

"Who?" said the voice at the other end trembling just a bit.

"Berguson. Leon Berguson. Ever hear of him?"

She changed the subject on a dime. "I'll take care of it, Mr. Denning. Did you know what was in the envelope?"

"Nope. That wasn't part of the deal, lady. Your sister paid me fifty-bucks fifteen days ago to find Berguson. When I tracked him down I was to tell your sister. I assume she connected with him and was to come over and give me the envelope, and next day I'd deliver it to what I was told was her address."

"I'm worried about my sister, Mr. Denning. She seems to have disappeared."

"Yeah? Well, I'm worried about bein' stiffed out of three hundred clams. Now, your sister's a big girl. Big enough to take care of herself, isn't she?"

"Please give me your address, Mr. Denning. I will mail you a check tonight for what Fredericka owes you."

14

"That would be nice, sister," I said rather sarcastically. I usually lose my patience with fuzzy dames after about two minutes. "Make it out to Cable Denning and send it to 6400 Franklin Avenue, Suite B, Hollywood. The sooner the better, lady. Now if you don't mind, I'm still trying to focus my eyes and nurse a headache that keeps batting home runs inside my skull."

"Yes, I'm sorry, Mr. Denning. Perhaps you may have a concussion and you should see your doctor."

"Miss Winston, the last time I saw a doctor was the day I was born. A doc's good for a broken arm and a kid's fever maybe, but not a grown up gumshoe like me."

We said good-bye and I hung up the phone like a man finally relieved of a pesky wife. I took another gulp of that cheap gin I keep buying from the liquor store down the street. I lit up another cigarette. I paced my office floor like a coyote looking for a way out of a pen. I was thumping my gin-soaked brain in an attempt to put more of the pieces together from a strange Tuesday that didn't turn out so well. In fact, I didn't enjoy it at all. I'm used to phony dames with phony names hiring me to do someone's dirty laundry. But Eleanor Winston sounded like she came from Camp Honest. Maybe her stupid sister *was* in trouble. But it wasn't my problem. Dames were always putting themselves up a creek over some dumb hoodlum who couldn't count past himself and used women for his own ends.

Finally the gin lulled me into that woozy numbness that rocks you like a slowly moving freight train. But when I got too horizontal, my head began to throb like I was standing inside a bass drum and the mallet was slamming against my brain. I kept trying to piece together the dark corners of today's little escapade. Now that I thought of it, not much of it made sense. I get hired by some beautiful broad to trace down a mysterious missing boyfriend who happens to be good with a blackjack. But even though I located him and watched him from a distance, I never saw Leon Berguson up close or front-on. The guy who whacked me could've been *anyone*! Then Fredericka Winston comes to my office, hands me an envelope to deliver to Lanterman Terrace. But...if she was going to meet me there, as she said, why didn't she take the damn envelope herself? And why would she hire *me* to deliver it to her boyfriend? A lot of stuff wasn't adding up. So maybe Leon Berguson was someone *else*, a business connection of some sort. Maybe it'd come back to me later, but I do seem to recall there *was* a woman at Lanterman Terrace. But what if it wasn't Fredericka Winston? And if not, just where *was* that flighty dame who left without paying me?

Finally, I slept a couple of hours. When I awoke, the insides of my mouth felt like all the cotton in Dixie had been stuffed into it. I rolled over to the bedside table to have another shot of that cure-all that said 17% grain alcohol on its label. The rest of my sleep was filled with what seemed like a replay of an old movie, somewhere between Charlie Chan and Buster Keaton, with dark, forbidden doors that opened wide and someone was pushing me from the rear to look inside. But it wasn't fun. It was a nightmare. You see, Charlie was murdering people and smiling at me at the same time. I tried to make like Buster with a stone face. But I couldn't. I ran, and a huge blackjack ran after me, some big hand whacking above my head like God with a fly swatter. But it mustn't hit me... I knew I couldn't take another blow without sprouting wings and singing *Alleluia*. Then it was morning.

I got up, brushed my teeth, and realized a front tooth was loose from the beating of a day ago. That explained the cut upper lip.

I tried to shave, but it was like cutting my beard with a lawn mower. The nerves in my face were acutely sensitive and my eyes were puffy enough to pose as Emmett the Clown. I heard someone rustling around out in my office.

"Boots? Is that you?" I asked.

A gruff, low-pitched voice answered, the kind you think oughtta belong to Popeye the Sailor Man. "Yep, you handsome son-of-a-bitch. Why in the hell don't you ever clean up in here? My mother would have called this a *pigsty*."

Boots Blake was in his mid-sixties and stood about five-six, wore a narrow-brimmed Stetson and cowboy boots. He was rather rotund and seemed to have been born in an old grayish cardigan sweater and black britches, always held up by the same old pair of beige suspenders. Pinned to the sweater was an old sheriff's badge, left over from the 1920's when he was a local constable in some one-horse town north of here, in San Luis Obispo County.

"So my mother raised a pig," I answered. I was the kinda guy who gumshoed alone in this life and had few friends. But I had a soft spot for old Boots. Maybe it was because he kept me connected to my Dad. If it wasn't for our chance meeting in Kathmandu when Dad suggested I look up this old friend, I may never have met Boots. Maybe, too, he reminded me of simpler times and before this damned war broke out last December. Or maybe he was the last honest man I knew. Anyway, he played sidekick and often I sent him on errands to snoop out someone or do some of my footwork. Boots liked that. He always smiled when he came back with the goods. He was a good man and I loved him.

Feeling somewhat refreshed, I came out and greeted Boots. I showed him the slowly deflating golf ball on the back of my head and told him my story. "But some pieces just don't fit, Boots. Like how and why did I get the cut lip? Getting hit from behind with a blackjack is one thing, but..."

"C'mon, kid," he said, even though I had turned forty-two last September. I knew that tone of voice. It was his way of being the father-figure I never had. "Let's find a park bench. Some fresh air and it'll all come back to ya."

We sat on an old green bench in Bronson Park watching feral cats play in the wild grasses under the oak trees. We sat near the entrance where we could see the red and yellow trolley cars ply their way down Bronson Avenue to connect with Sunset Boulevard a mile or so below. The old folks, I reflected, had simple formulas for getting to the heart of things. And that was exactly what I needed....simple.

"So it seems that only *part* of my memory is intact," I told Boots. The older man squinted his eyes, revisiting an old mysterious story somewhere in his memory banks.

"Once I traced a bunch of shady lookin' characters up to a house hidden in the hills above Morro Bay. Oh, this musta been back in the late '20s or so." He was chewing on the remnants of a cheap Roi Tan he had smoked earlier. When he wasn't smoking cigars, he chewed tobacco and his browned teeth proved it had been a long-standing habit. "Seems there was a burglary ring operatin' down in the town. So once I located the cabin, I began to check on who owned it and who was livin' in it at the time. "and then what, Boots?" I asked. Well, now, as ol' Art Beatle woulda said, 'Pshaw!' 'cause ain't nobody lived there in that cabin and the owner lived here in the city."   "So you're suggesting I find out who owns or rents 2433 Lanterman Terrace?"

"Yep. Good place to start." He tossed his cigar butt and bit off a plug of chewing tobacco and tucked it in his cheek. "Do ya wanna hear the rest of my story or not?"

"Of course, Boots! What? And not learn from one of the oldest and best sleuths in the business?" I chuckled.

"Now don't ya go laughin' at me, Cable, just 'cause I'm an old man with half the sense I used ta have," he admonished me. So he continued his story: "Seemed to me these guys was up to no good, no matter what they did. So I began to do some spyin' of my own. The place was like a den of iniquity and dark goins on. An' not always the same faces came and went. Some, yep—others, nope. Then one day I happened to see them escort an older man out of one of their cars towards the cabin. But something was very peculiar about this fellow."

19

"And what would that be? Now, don't tell me. It was someone they got paid to bump off."

"Now, young smart aleck...keep shut. Who's tellin' this story...you or me here?"

"Sorry, Boots, I was, uh, trying to hurry it along a little."

My old friend gave me a dirty look and continued. "The stealin' and fencin' stuff was just a side occupation to keep them boys from bein' too bored with their remote location. What they was really in for was the old kidnap-and-ransom game."

A light went on inside my still aching head. I shuffled through my own case histories with clients like a lost thumb and forefinger flicking through playing cards. "You know....you might have something there, Boots. Would you do me a favor? Go to a real estate office in the area. See what they know. Go to City Hall and find 2433 Lanterman Terrace on the tax records in the assessor's office. You never know what we'll find." Then I got up from the bench. "I have to hunt down an errant husband this afternoon. I'll let you off so you can take the trolley to Silver Lake."

Boots and I agreed we would connect by phone in the evening. I drove him to the trolley connection and went about my business tracking down George Heard. He had obviously been philandering with his secretary. Mrs. Heard was not happy about it, so she paid me to pinpoint times, dates, locations...even take a handsome photo with my Kodak box camera. I wasn't too bad as a photographer, but not that good either. Seems my hand wasn't too steady. Maybe it was too much booze and cigarettes. It sure wasn't too many women. The pickings had been pretty sparse lately. Having a great time with a woman without getting entangled in all the emotional crap people go through was the challenge these days. For me, it was about a pretty face, nice figure, tits and pussy. A good time for the night and no expectations tomorrow. That's what I had become. It didn't even hurt if she threw me out after the booze wore off the next morning and I never saw her again. But I always liked it if she could speak well of herself and be somewhat articulate. But then again, I wasn't the best entertainment for the buck in that department, either.

It was around ten when I got back to my office. A man who works, eats and sleeps in the same few rooms is subject to a lonely life, especially being a private dick. Only your clients and the very few friends you have turn out to be your social circle. I hadn't gone out bar hopping since my middle thirties, and hook-up dances and the meat market were an anathema to me. But once in a while I got lucky and met a dame who wanted what I wanted. No strings, just good company and a fun roll in the sack.

I opened my door and went directly to my desk where a third of a bottle of gin beckoned to me. I poured a long one and sat in my comfy old desk chair. I was wondering if Boots had called, when the phone rang.

"Hello..." I said in a tired voice.

"Mr. Denning, this is Eleanor Winston again. Are you going to be in your office for a while? I know it's late, but I'm in the neighborhood and I would like to bring by your check...the money my sister owes you."

While that in itself sounded tempting because my funds were running low, I balked at the thought of another screwed up dame telling me her sorrows and the plight of her now-missing sister. It had been too long of a day. "Frankly, Miss Winston, it's after ten o'clock...I'm not an all-night diner, ya know!"

I could hear her snicker at the other end. "That was cute. I never heard that before...it'll only take a few minutes."

"All the same, it's been a long day and my head still aches from your sister's boyfriend's blackjack or whatever it was that hit me."

I could feel the wheels turn in her brain over the telephone. She hesitated, but I could hear her whimpering. The oldest trick in the book! "I was hoping...hoping you would see me, Mr. Denning...oh! I am so distressed! Fredericka is still missing and there is no trace...please, Mr. Denning, I need your help!"

Like the male chump I am, I fell for that old line. There's something about a woman crying which unbalances a guy. It comes from some alien reservoir in her, another tool in her arsenal of control tactics. And the less-couth gender is a perfect patsy for that kind of strategy. "Why don't you go to the police, Miss Winston. That's what they *do* for your tax dollars."

"I can't...and I can't explain it over the telephone! Please, please ...just for a few moments, won't you see me, I ask you, Mr. Denning?"

"Alright, Miss Winston, where are you?"

"In a phone booth across the street from your building."

"Well, seeing that you're that close, come on up. Second floor, Suite B." She hung up and I bolstered myself for the visit with another round of rotten gin. My eyes darted across my desk like a cat following the movement of a busy fly. I needed to focus. My brain strained and my head pounded. So I lit up a cigarette, sat back and waited. Soon there was a knock at the outer door. "Come in."

I wasn't prepared for the exquisite looks and body of this female creature. Even through my foggy brain and the lousy past two days, her entrance hit me like a dump truck full of concrete. The dame was stunning!

"Mr. Denning?" she intoned as she came toward me. I got up from behind my desk and went to greet her. She offered me her hand and I felt like a goddess had sent lightning bolts down to my shoes. Her eyes were a penetrating green-blue and her red hair was full and excellently coiffed. She had that look of elegant maturity—I figured her for about 35. Her hands were strong but delicate while the fingernails were perfectly manicured and long, tapering to points a full half-inch or more from her fingertips. She wore a light-green suit, her ample figure filling it out in all the right places and cream colored shoes, open at the toe. "Thank you for seeing me. I'm sorry for disturbing you." She looked around at the helter-skelter rooms I called home. "Do you live here?"

"You're always saying that, aren't you?" I said as I released her hand.

"Saying what?"

"That you're sorry about something or other...I read you as that type of dame."

"Well, I guess I've been imposing on you a lot lately and—"

"—but here you are, Miss. Winston, and I'm glad to meet you." I said, that really being a paramount understatement considering this woman was a *dish*. "Please, sit down."

She sat opposite me, those beautiful, intense eyes studying me. "I suppose you think I'm just another unhinged female, don't you?"

"Well, I wouldn't say that, Miss Winston...I am assuming you are *miss?* ...no, I would not say you are just another anything but a very strikingly beautiful woman who I'll bet has a few brains swirling around underneath all that lovely red hair."

She blushed. I was sure those lines were not strange to her ears or that most men she met were on the make for her the second they saw her. "Why thank you, Mr. Denning. On a day like today, it's most welcomed. And actually it's *Mrs.* My husband is a scientist working on a project in England at the moment."

That disappointing news always hits a man where he lives. To even get a hint that a woman he might desire is unavailable to him, changes the vibration of the room, not to mention that it reduces his ego and libido into childhood places. "I see...." I said, trying to cover my tone of voice to maintain my business-like manner. "So....what can I do for you, Mrs. Winston?"

She took an embroidered handkerchief out of her purse and dabbed her eyes. It looked to me like she was the genuine article. And these weren't crocodile tears, either. I'd seen it before. Something was eating at her from a place deep down, like a consuming worm fighting its way to the surface. If she didn't take care of it, purge it out, throw it away, it would devour her, rob her

24

of her youth and beauty, cause her to sink to the place where all gorgeous babes go when life hands them a hammer blow in the gut and it ricochets right to the heart. "I want you to work for me, Mr. Denning." She reached again into her purse and withdrew a check. "Here's eight-hundred dollars. Three of it is what you said Fredericka owed you, the other five is for you to help me find her and bring her home safely to me."

I reached over and took the check from this fancy dish sitting across from me. Yep, eight hundred smackers alright. But I did have professional ethics. " Uh, before I can take a case on, Mrs. Winston, I need to know the boundaries. There are rules to every game. I need to know if you're on the level with me, who you are, who your sister really is, what she's up to, who's involved in her life and what danger to my person would such an undertaking entail? Remember, I've already got a knot on my head."

"I'm sorry. I didn't realize..."

"There you go again. *You* don't have to be personally sorry. If you'll pardon my saying so, let's just cut out the polite crap and get to it, okay?

"I...I'm not sure what you mean..."

I could tell my words were more coarse than she was used to. But I had to be me. Take it or leave it, sister. That was how I thought, acted, I had no apology for the hard-boiled reality I existed in. "Well, you see, Mrs. Winston, we need to get something straight if I'm going to work for you. I speak L.A. street language, the roughest dialect of the people, the poor creatures who claw with their fingernails against the glass to eke out a living, not the rich and insulated who live in ivory palaces and think their crap doesn't stink. I'm talking about the hard way, the world I live and work in, what people are *really* about, who are born, live, love and die forgotten on some slab at the county morgue. And maybe, just maybe, there'll be a little happiness along the way for these simple folk. That's who I am. Now, if you want to get up and leave, find a high-priced private dick to find your sister in the lofty inner sanctum of her secret world—I understand." I stopped. I couldn't believe I found myself ranting at this beautiful young woman across from me. "So now you know my raw underbelly. How's it feel?"

Instead of cowering, slapping me in the face or just leaving the room, Eleanor Winston was crying. But these weren't tears of self-pity, I had reached a place where she dared not wander before. Now it struck a chord. "I guess I deserve that. It is true, I have been insulated all of my life." Then she looked deep into me and I knew she knew she had penetrated a wounded place in me so wide that I would never live long enough to measure the pain. "But what you said was honest and truthful, Mr. Denning. I am not offended, but I am now all the more resolved to have you in my employ."

"You're kiddin'...why me?" Just then the phone rang. "Yeah, it's late...." It was Boots.

"Where the hell've you been, Cable?"

"I told you, tracking down an errant husband. The way I saw it, Mr. George Heard had the better end of the deal. The secretary is a cream puff, probably ten years his junior."

Boots laughed over the phone. "Ha! So, that's what ya been doin', eh? Did ya snap the all-important photo?"

"I sure did, Boots. My client will have her money's worth, I suspect. So what did you find out about you-know-what?" I didn't want Eleanor Winston to get wind of what Boots was about to reveal to me.

"*Nobody lives in the damn house* on Lanterman. It hasn't been lived in for over a year."

So that's why the light switch didn't work. The news came in like the tide at Malibu, bringing in the debris humans foul the sea with. All the garbage that lies beneath, created on the beaches of greed and deceit. "Not surprised, Boots. Good work. Say, you know, I've got a client here just now. Can I call you in the morning? It's been a hell of a day. My feet are sore and I'm almost out of gin and cigarettes." I laughed. "Hell of a note, eh Boots?"

There was a knowing pause at the other end of the line. "Is this...this *client*... of the female kind by any chance, you dog?"

"Yep. Tomorrow morning, Boots. Good-night, old boy." I hung up and looked over at Eleanor Winston. I could tell on her face she disapproved of my smoking and drinking. I knew what she was thinking, that a man like me should be healthy and athletic, playing tennis at the country club, driving a custom Maserati with the top down and having a cocktail at 3:00 after a lunch of salad and lightly grilled salmon. "Sorry about that, business you know," I said, looking for a reaction.

"Now it's you who are apologizing. I assure you it's not necessary, Mr. Denning. Now, do you wish to know more about me before you take me as a client?"

We talked until well after midnight, mostly her answering stupid questions that I asked. She didn't break stride under my scrutiny and answered in all the right ways. I found myself like a helpless boxer in the ring, being punched by a fist that somehow didn't hurt, but something was munching at my heart, melting through corridors of hardened acid and old memories. She battered me with that sultry feminine voice, her truthful demeanor and those blue-green eyes that glowed out at me like beacons in a foggy night. "For a protected dame, you talk a pretty good talk, sister. So, for those five-hundred greenbacks you gave me, I guess I'm in it until the fat lady cries."

"Sings." She laughed. "It's until the fat lady *sings*," she corrected me.

"Oops! So I get my metaphors mixed up now and then."

When she laughed, that smile lit up the whole damn room. Then she got back down to brass tacks. "I know it's late, I must go soon. Just one more question, if I may. Where do we start?"

I looked straight at her and took my last sip of gin for the night. "Don't you know? Women are intuitive. Tell me, Mrs. Winston, if you don't mind, I've always wanted to know. What's the basic essence in a woman...that stuff that makes her tick?"

She looked at me surprised, as if I had walked into the women's bathroom at the Biltmore when she was on the pot with her pink panties down to her ankles. "What...what a strange question, Mr. Denning. I don't know if I'm prepared to answer that...it's...it's probably many different things for many different women."

"So, what about you? What quality comes up and bites you in the…uh…when you're thinking about your husband, for instance?"

She blushed a little but forced a smile to let me know she was still in the game. "Nurturing. I think that's the most important gift a woman has."

"And you?" I probed.

"Me, too." She got up from her chair. I came around and helped her put on her coat. "So what's the first step in finding Fredericka?"

"There's a lot more going on here. I'm not even sure your sister's in danger. What if she just ran off with Berguson?

"Do you really believe that?" she asked.

"No, I don't," I answered matter-of-factly. Then I smiled and laughed as our eyes met. I scratched my head. "How to kick things off, hmm…maybe we should hire a psychic and get a head start. You know, a madam this or madam that who wears the wrap-around bandana with the crystal pin on the forehead?"

Eleanor Winston's eyes widened and her mouth flew open like she was preparing to swallow a bowl filled with goldfish. "*You* are psychic! How did you know? That's exactly what I had planned to do tomorrow. Would you like to come?"

"I was kidding." Yeah…even though my experience with Madam Palladino back in 1927 was right on the money about the whereabouts of the Golden Capsule, most so-called psychics just put on a sideshow fashioned to entrap the unsuspecting wallet or coin purse into giving up some dough. Frankly, I was surprised a class dame like Mrs. Winston put any stock in that stuff. "Thanks all the same, but I think I'll skip it."

"Well, just in case. Her name is Madam Zorrie Robles, there's a walk-down entrance near Mexican Village on 5th and Olvera. My appointment is at two-o'clock."

I escorted her to the door. She offered me her hand again, but this time the gin had numbed the distance to my feet and all I felt was a nice soft hand. "Well, good-night, Mrs. Winston. I won't be able to start on your case for another day or two, just so you know and don't get the idea I'm living high off your money."

A look of desperation ran across her face. "Why wait so long? Poor Fredericka is out there somewhere, God knows where or in what condition! Can't you hurry, I beg you!" She looked like a newborn puppy about to lick my face if I said no, so I took a deep breath and made a rare concession.

"I told you, there's always the cops. That's what they allegedly get paid for. But I already have a lead. Actually, I suppose I can do some nosing around tomorrow afternoon."

"Thank you." With that Eleanor Winston turned and I opened the door for her. "Good-night, Mr. Denning."

I looked after her. Suddenly I got a kind of chill that turned my insides into five kinds of Jell-O. "Oh, I'd better walk you to your car. This late at night and all...."

"Thank you. That's very considerate."

We stepped into the night air. It smelled of diesel and garbage. At a bus stop across the street I was sure that I saw a figure dart back into that world of shadows where ghosts, lovers and bad guys hide out. I grabbed

Eleanor Winston's arm and we walked. "But my car is the other way, Mr. Denning," she informed me.

"Keep walking, toots. Don't look around, stay on my inside. I think there's a character waiting for you across the street. Tell me...and don't stop walking...is your car across the street by the bus stop?"

"Why, yes. How did you know?"

"Just a hunch. Maybe it's nothin'."

But as we turned the corner another man was coming our way, like a dark specter from a horror movie. Under a street lamp I could see him reach into his left pocket for something and I knew it wasn't his favorite yo-yo. Quick as a wink I pushed Eleanor Winston into an apartment building doorway and drew my own gun. As the mysterious stranger walked by, he saw the glint of my .38 and hurried on. I told Mrs. Winston to stay put as I gave chase to the man in the black leather coat. By the time I got around the corner he had crossed the street and joined the other man in the shadows. Together they ran east, toward Western Avenue. I pursued them for a minute or two, but the booze and cigarettes slowed me down. Finally I turned around and went back to get Eleanor Winston.

"Thank goodness...you're alright! Who was that man? Was he after us?"

"Not us...*you*! And he had a buddy waiting in the shadows by your car."

It was all too much and suddenly this beautiful babe collapsed into my arms, holding on to me, shaking like a little girl who's fallen through the ice on the skating rink. "Oh, forgive me! That's why I can't go to the police.

You never asked me about that tonight. But it's more complicated than I know...or can tell you."

"I suggest you'd better start tryin' just about now."

She reached into her coat pocket and withdrew a handkerchief. She dabbed her eyes and then looked at me with those stock-and-trade blue-green lamps of hers, now obscured in the partial darkness of the doorway "Please, give me a moment."

"I didn't ask about you going to the cops because at the time there seemed no need to ask it. Plus I needed the money. But now I don't know. I think you've been holding out on me. I think you're running me around the barber's pole, and maybe...just maybe...those two guns out there weren't for you, but to get me out of the way."

"No! Please! It isn't true! I didn't tell you...I didn't tell you one thing...one thing...oh, now I'm so ashamed, you asked me only for the truth and I deceived you—but what I didn't tell you was that my husband has been kidnapped and forcibly taken to Europe. Fredericka and I thought Leon Berguson was the contact to help us free Carlton." I watched as this quick thinking dame turned the old story, with a quick twist into new, like a sorceress of alchemy changing the old metal to gold.

"So what was in the envelope?" I asked.

"Money. Lots of it. A down payment to guarantee the safe return of my husband. But Fredericka and I were betrayed and I think we're dealing with some very sinister people."

"So I get a lump on my noggin and a split lip over a money exchange? Somehow it doesn't add up, sister." I was doing some calculating of my own and what kept coming up queer and didn't quite fit was the name of Carlton Winston, her husband. "So what exactly does your husband do, Mrs. Winston."

"I'm not exactly certain. He works for the United States Military & the Scientific Research and Development Program. I think it's part of the Secret Service. All of his work is classified and I am never privy to it."

"Well, don't stop now, it's just starting to get interesting. What other new things am I destined to find out when you turn on your charm and truth machine at the same time?"

"I know...I must seem like an awful person to you just now...and I've betrayed your trust as a client..."

"So far you're battin' five-hundred, sister. Wanna go for six? I'm not known to be a very patient man." I put my gun in my pocket but stuck it in her ribs. "Now move, Eleanor Winston, or whoever you are. Over there...toward your car." We crossed the street and headed for the bus stop where her car was parked.

"No...please...they'll kill me...and you!" she cried.

"Or anyone else connected to your husband through you or your sister?"

"Yes! Yes! Take me back up to your office! Please!"

"Not tonight, sister. You see, one thing I didn't tell you about me. I was hoping you'd see it. I'm a straight shooter. Can you understand that? Nobody's perfect but *truth* is the one thing I need to have around me, kinda like a good fairy who sticks because I'm true to her, the one thing I've needed all my life but always end up with dames like you who'll sell their grandmother if the big bad wolf doesn't come in time." She was frozen and

33

speechless at my tirade. I urged her toward her car and I helped her get into it. I threw her purse in after her. "One more thing, you write me another check tomorrow...for three-hundred bucks to even the score. I'll tear up the one you gave me tonight. I don't need your five-hundred clams that bad, lady."

I slammed the car door and walked away. I didn't turn back to see, but I could hear her car start up and she pulled away into the Los Angeles night.

I got back up to my office and brushed my teeth. I was still shaking. I wasn't sure if it was the booze or the anger that woman had brought out in me. I took one last swig of gin to kill the bottle and fell into bed.

Chapter 2

THE WINDS OF SANTA ANA

I woke up hot and sweating. A tall, thin gypsy woman had been chasing me. She kept pointing her finger over my head, admonishing me like a schoolboy who had just dipped a classmate's pigtails into an inkwell. There was an incessant ringing in my ears and it wouldn't leave me alone. I slugged my pillow hoping it would stop. But it didn't. The gypsy was telling me to be careful as the ring grew louder and drove me nuts. She kept saying I must protect Eleanor Winston from some horrible fate, the kind that hangs around dark hallways, the kind you can feel in your bones but can't see. You can taste its cold venom in your mouth because it lives inside of you and its bite is fatal. Only you're not sure, because something was planted in your head a long time ago and it's eating you from the inside out like an army of potato bugs gnawing at the back of your skull.

Finally I came to. That incessant ringing was my phone. I staggered to my desk to answer it. "Yeah, Cable Denning here..."

"Where've you been, you hard-livin' ladies' man! I've been callin' you for an hour...and my ulcer's killin' me worryin' about you." It was Boots. My head began to clear enough to know I wasn't dreaming anymore.

"Sorry, Boots, I got in late and had quite a time with that Winston dame."

"Why use a hotel...you coulda saved a bundle and taken her to your own bed..."

"Well, ...no, Boots, it wasn't like that. She stayed late. We talked business. I escorted her to her car and on the way we ran into a couple of pretty mean characters packing iron. They ran when they saw my .38, but these guys looked like they meant business, Boots, and wore long black leather overcoats. Didn't look American to me."

"Maybe they weren't, Cable. I'd be careful if I was you...the war and all now, ya know."

I tried to light a cigarette but my fingers were shaking, so in disgust I threw it on the floor. I looked around the room for a drink. I remembered I had killed the bottle the night before. "You can forget about Lanterman Terrace. It was just a pick-up spot. Seems our dear Mrs. Winston and her sister were handing off some dough to these mugs. The husband works for the scientific end of the Secret Service, far as I can gather."

"The *husband,* eh? That's enough tumble weed right there! Whatta ya usin' fer brains, son? So, wait now. Ya say ya got conked on the skull for deliverin' the money? Somethin' doesn't add up here," Boots growled.

"That's what I said to Mrs. Winston last night just before I dismissed her as a client and booted her into her car."

"You mean you're off the case? Unsolved? That's not like you, Cable. What'd she do...piss ya off?" he asked sarcastically.

"Lied to me. Or at the very least, concealed important facts until the mugs showed up and panicked her into spilling everything."

"Now you lost 'er. Hmm...so it's back to chasing down naughty husbands, wives and lovers, eh?

"Yeah, I know, Boots. I think I had a soft spot for the dish anyway and didn't wanna mix business with pleasure."

"Too bad. You needed the money." Boots cleared his raspy throat. "You got the pain, so ya gonna get some of the pleasure?"

"Nope, I'm sitting this one out, Boots. I got a bad feeling about what may be dangling at the other end of that line. You know me, Boots. I'm a simple guy. A quart of good gin, a pack of cigarettes, a good woman now and then…a few decent clients…you know, what else could a man want?"

"A hell of lot more, Cable, especially you! You're a smart one…a cut above most of 'em, man. Ya should think more of yourself and put a halt to the booze and too many smokes. Both of 'em will kill ya…"

I was only half-listening as I saw a telegram slip under my front office door. "I've gotta glue myself together, Boots. And then get the film on George Heard down to the drugstore and get it developed. Talk to you tomorrow."

"Too bad. I was rather intrigued by that Winston case. We're needin' some excitement in our lives, Cable."

"Well, I'm not sure that's the kind I'm looking for. Something else will turn up. It always does. Talk later, Boots." I hung up the phone feeling like mushrooms were starting to grow in the pit of my stomach. I didn't know why, but all of a sudden I felt guilty about last night, shouting at the dame when maybe she was actually on the level. I knew in my gut I was being too personal and unprofessional…bringing my own resentments into the arena of my work. I needed a drink. I would stop by George's Liquor store on my way to drop off the film. Buy some more Lucky Strikes, too.

I walked slowly toward the telegram there on the floor like a man on his way to the gallows. I had this funny feeling that whatever was in that piece of paper would change my life. If I only knew then how prophetic that was. My stiff body creaked as I bent down to pick it up. I opened it....my hands still shaking from too much booze and cigarettes the night before. Not to mention my nerves from the scathing anger I directed at Eleanor Winston.

It was semi-light in my office and my eyes were still sensitive to light. I went to the window by my desk, the one that over-looked Franklin Avenue. I noticed the palms across the way were blowing violently in the wind. I opened my window. A blast of hot air came through, blowing papers off my desk. The Santa Anas had arrived. Almost every year in late summer, the winds blew over from the scorched mountains to the east. This was the time of year when housing developments tucked up above Laurel Canyon, went up in smoke. Movie stars, corporate moguls, and the rich and famous were equalized in that moment, when all the things they identified with perished in flame and ash. Yeah, how stupid of the county to let people build homes up there in those firetrap canyons. Ah, but that was how greed and money worked...otherwise known as 'progress'...and they all lived in the House That Jack Built. Follow the money trail, I always say.

I opened the telegram and I squinted my eyes as I read: *Mr. Denning (stop) please, forgive behavior (stop)*

both of ours (stop) Is there room for amends? (stop) El-
eanor Winston.

All I knew in that moment was that I had to be there with her at 2:00 p.m. when she visited the fortune teller, the one I dreamed about last night, *Madam Zorrie Robles*, 5th near Olvera. To avoid paying for downtown public parking, I paid a dime and walked three blocks. The Santa Ana winds blew dust, paper, dirt and debris across the streets as the hot air caught my lungs off guard and I had to cough. The joint Eleanor Winston had described looked like the entrance to a tomb with the familiar palm painted in black and white above the transom. As I descended the stairs, the smell of old liquor and stale tobacco along with the usual street smells that you get accustomed to. I had seen a lot of seedy joints in my time, but this one ranked right up there. There was a bell. I rang it and the door buzzed and I entered. But once I got inside, the place suddenly transformed into a pleasant parlor with occult paintings on the wall and a caption under a rather odd piece entitled *Sacred Geometry*. I did recognize old Diogenes handing the child a glowing light of wisdom from the palm of his hand.

No one else was around, it seemed. It was almost two-o'clock and there was no sign of Mrs. Winston. I was about to smoke when I thought better. The room I stood in seemed to have a sweetness about it, probably some kind of aromatic incense. Why corrupt it with my smelly weeds?

Just then a tall, dark-haired woman appeared from behind some curtains at the far end of the waiting room. She possessed dark penetrating eyes, the kind that lock on to you and you wish they hadn't. I got the feeling she saw a naked man standing before her with a sheepish smile.

"Yes? May I help you?" she intoned in a rather low-pitched voice that kind of went with her body.

"Uh, yes, my name is Cable Denning, and I gather you must be Miss Robles. We have a client in common, I believe…Eleanor Winston?"

The tall dark-eyed dame flashed me a vague smile as if some other thought was rattling around in her brain. Her full lips shined with a pink-orange lipstick. "Yes. I am expecting Eleanor to be here any minute." Then she studied my face. "Won't you come to my table and have a seat? I have something to tell *you*, Mr. Denning, free of charge."

As stingy as I was, that was the best part of her offer. I followed her into a small room that was quite handsomely appointed with curtains for wallpaper in shades of forest green, magenta, a rather warm yellow-orange and a pleasing blue. On a small table sat the most striking crystal ball I'd ever seen. and The candlelight that bounced all around it made it almost seem to have life.

"Quite a set-up you have here, Madam Zorrie, if I may call you that." A very different picture to my experience with Madam Palladino, I thought. She was a short Italian with an unimposing atmosphere and definitely interested in getting paid…but she was plugged in to something alright and I guess that's what counts in the end.

"It fits what I have to do in this life, Mr. Denning. What are you living *your* life for?"

I chuckled to cover my surprise at her rather audacious question. "Uh, me? I...I, uh, well, that's a good question, Madam Zorrie. I don't suppose we're born with all the pieces in their right place. It takes time to sort out what you like and what you feel you're cut out for. I mean, a simple guy like me came with limited credentials. As I figure it, I could've been either a plasterer or a private dick. I chose the latter so I could pick my own hours, I suppose," I said that in a slightly sarcastic tone, hoping she'd get the hint I was talking tongue-in-cheek. But she was a serious dame and pursued the topic like a bulldog hanging on to a bone.

"You're one of those displaced persons, Mr. Denning. You are more intelligent than most, but settle for what you have because you don't believe in yourself sufficiently. You're afraid to grab the bull by the horns, so to speak. Men like you are pitiful in a way. You feel sorry for yourself a lot of the time, and your ego is damaged enough to make you turn to alcohol or other drugs to diminish the pain you can't understand inside yourself."

The woman was hitting the bull's eye on all cylinders, and it was getting a bit personal, not to mention uncomfortable. But I retained my polite demeanor. "Now, just how would you know that, Madam Zorrie? Is that included under the heading of a palmist's clairvoyance?"

She went to a sink nearby and washed her hands. After she wiped them, she approached her crystal ball and stroked it gently with her long, thin fingers. "Actually, yes." She took a deep breath and seemed to tune into me. "Now, why was I chasing you?" she asked and I almost fell off my seat.

41

"Wait a minute! How...how can you possibly know about a dream I dreamed last night? And even though I never met you, you were in it."

She remained calm and even flashed me a warm smile. "We're all connected, Mr. Denning. You, me, Eleanor, Fredericka, the country, the planet, even the universe...you cannot make waves in your pond without me feeling the ripples. No one is ever separated from another except in thought."

That one went a little over my head. "If you say so, lady. But I still can't figure the dream stuff. There are a lot of folks I would definitely not want to be connected with. Are you sure of that crystal ball's accuracy on that count?" I was putting her on.

She laughed. "I like you, Mr. Denning. You're talking about human personalities, behavioral aberrations. You deal a lot with people whose genetics or brains are not well, or their early environment warped them to step outside the norm of society."

"Boy, you hit the bull's eye with that, sister," I said, amazed at the woman's brain. "Well, now that you've probed my twisted internal wrappings, uh...what do you see for the future, if I...uh...may be so bold?"

She bent over the crystal ball once again. I noticed the color on her face changed and the rouge had faded a bit. "I would guess you were born in September, Mr. Denning. Perhaps somewhere around the middle?"

"Now how could you know that? You're amazing, lady. I was born on September the 13th right at the turn of our century, 1900.

"That Virgo in you is stubborn, and you probably have an addictive behavior trait. You must watch that.

But as far as your future, you are just entering a new astrological cycle, new people, new experiences, extraordinary events..." She studied the crystal ball intensely. "You will be involved in a work so highly unique that I cannot define it.... just be aware that it will take you into great danger. You may or may not survive this one, Mr. Denning. I don't mean to be intrusive and I'm not a doomsayer, but I must report what I see. That is my truth and I always dwell in truth."

"You should've married *me* in a past life, Madam Zorrie...I mean, truth is the one code I stick to. In fact, that's why I got pissed at Mrs. Winston last night..."

"Please, don't be hard on her. She's a gem of a person, and as you know, a beautiful and intelligent woman. Go easy with her."

"Well, I'm afraid it's a little late for that. I blew up at her last night when a couple of mugs in black leather trench coats and packing heat, started hunting us down right outside my office on Franklin. I found out she had been concealing important..."

Just then the bell rang and Madam Zorrie put her finger to her lips to hush me. She exited. I became nervous having to face Eleanor Winston again. But some things you have to swallow.

She looked beautiful when she entered. She had the kind of look about her that movie stars have in close-ups, when the luminous gauzy-haze makes you want to take her home with you. She wore a white skirt, pleated at the knee, with a black silk blouse, black patent leather heels and a stunning but simple emerald necklace to complement her lovely red hair. The blouse was cut so that her fine breasts could come out for a breather if she happened to bend over immodestly.

Her surprise to see me was evident. "Mr. Denning! What...what and how did you...Zorrie...?"

"You did give me the time and place of your meeting with Madam Zorrie here, and after your kind telegram this morning...well, Mrs. Winston, I thought I may be of some assistance to you," I said on my best behavior, "and I'm quite pleased to see you again. I might have been a little rough on you last night."

She smiled. "And I am glad...as well as surprised...to find you here with my friend Zorrie. I would have been here sooner, but I foolishly took the bus. I assume you two have become acquainted. I hope so."

"Oh, yeah, I find her most entertaining and she was on target on a couple of counts. I can see why people respect her abilities."

Madam Zorrie chuckled. "Look out for that Virgo charm. That earth sign will do you in if you're not careful." Then she grew very serious and asked both of us to sit opposite her at the little table in the middle of her small room. "Eleanor...do I have your permission to have Mr. Denning present? Somehow the two of you are *already* embroiled in the things that are unfolding."

"Of course, Zorrie. That was my original intention before Mr. Denning and I had the altercation of last evening..."

"We've got to skip over all that and get on with it. There isn't time.

I sat there with the women like a kid in a house of mirrors at a carnival. I didn't know what reflection would be thrown at me next. Who would I see? And if I looked, what demon in me would be telling me to get up and run, telling me if I stayed next to Eleanor Winston I would lose control, find myself running through the maze of mirrors, screaming for an old self that felt comfortable....and alive. Something told me I didn't have much of a chance at that, either. As I saw it, those goons last night were just previews of coming attractions, an opener for a very long ball game that was about to be pitched by a clever carny named Madame Zorrie. I nervously inter-locked my fingers and twisted the ring on my pinky. Why was it so damn hot in here?

"Eleanor....I have to tell you. We must put some light around Fredericka. She is in terrible danger." Madam Zorrie closed her eyes for a moment as if she were thrashing around in those pitch-black corners where evil and specters hang out. "The key...the key is a medium-sized man with curly dark hair, he stole....or he took some money from you..."

"Yeah, Berguson, Leon Berguson, the strong arm who hit me over the head the night I was supposed to deliver the envelope of money to Fredericka on Lanterman Terrace."

"Perhaps," Madam Zorrie muttered under her breath.

"What can we do?" "I feel so helpless just sitting here, Zorrie."

But the tall gypsy maintained her cool. "Sometimes we need advance information before we can proceed. We need a match lit in a dark room so we can see who's in it."

I thought that pretty smart of the gypsy dame. If she proved right, I could use her in my own trade to sniff out the skunks who hide out in the dark places no one else would dare enter....except chumps like me. Nothing like a little insight before you go out that door to set yourself up as a patsy for murder.

Nervously, Madam Zorrie got up from her chair and again went over to the sink and washed her hands. Either she was very clean or she was picking up vibes she didn't want to keep. While her back was turned, Eleanor Winston touched my hand and whispered to me. "Thank you for being here." If we were in a movie theatre in the dark and she did that, I would've grabbed her hand and held on to it like a teenaged boy with his first tidal wave of testosterone.

Madam Zorrie came back and sat down. I noticed the candles flicker like someone was gently blowing over them. The psychic was using those long tapered fingers of hers to decipher what the spirits...or whatever they were...might be communicating. Finally, she looked up, her eyes widened, and a great perplexity covered her face. It kind of looked like she had wet her pants and was just as surprised as anyone else in the room.

"Whatever the cause of all this terrible trouble...it isn't from *the here*...I am honestly baffled."

" What's, uh, *the here* mean, Madam Zorrie?" I asked, sure that I knew the answer.

"The earth....this planet."

Mrs. Winston opened her mouth and looked at me, but no words came. Well, I sighed, here we go again, right into a science fiction movie. "Well, Madam Zorrie," I said at last, attempting to keep a light mood. "You certainly have a colorful way of...of...ah... describing what you see. Are you talking about little green men from outer space?"

She stared at me unblinking. "...From other dimensions, Mr. Denning. You see, there is an invisible curtain, and nothing more, between this world and other dimensions of existence."

"Well, the religionists might give you a rough time on that one."

"Be that as it may, religion is a way for people to find faith in higher things. Everyone travels a different pathway."

"So what pathway are we going to follow?" Mrs. Winston was getting a little nervous with so much patter going on in the room. Maybe she was an action kind of dame after all. Sure, she had the body for it, I thought. Maybe it was the kind of action where clothes somehow come off in the darkness of a bedroom and the man wonders who's on top, or when he wakes up in the morning he wonders if he dreamed it all. The excitement wasn't commonplace, and your sore body tells you something good must have happened. Yeah, and then there's the message in lipstick smudged onto the bathroom mirror when you stumble in on the morning after...*I think I love you*, it says, *see you next time*...

"My advice is to track down the man who stole the envelope of money. The spirits see this Leon Berguson as holding the key that unlocks the next phase of the mystery. But you must act quickly. Time is of the essence, in several ways, and not just because of Fredericka's safety."

"You mean there's more? This sounds like one of those detective novels that're filled with levels and layers until, until—"

"—precisely, layers and levels. I will tell both of you now. There are some very powerful players in this game." Then she turned to Mrs. Winston. "Eleanor, what was Fredericka's connection to Berguson?"

The lady next to me blushed. "She was his lover. Fredericka never knows what she wants. She got mixed up with this character at a party Carlton threw some months ago, before he...he was abducted. Leon gave me the creeps. You know the type, knowledgeable, in command, knows all the tricks in the book, and had the right words to captivate and woo my sister into a romantic liaison. So she fell in love with him."

"And then what happened?" I asked, in perfect detective tone.

"Ah...well, they were a hot item for a while. Then Leon Berguson disappeared. Fredericka was miserable and wanted to find him. She didn't have much money, so I told her I would help her out. She could hire a private detective to find him."

"Enter...detective Denning. I uncover the bloke, but there's something else in the mix, isn't there? Suddenly there's this mysterious reason to deliver an envelope of dough to Berguson at an abandoned house on Lanterman Terrace in Silverlake. Only Berguson doesn't know the guy Fredericka hired is a chump and believes what she told him...that it's all a routine, safe delivery when he walks into a blackjack in a semi-dark room with the front door open. When I finally come to, my wallet's still in my breast pocket but the envelope is gone...along with Leon Berguson and your sister, if she was ever there. Suddenly it dawns on me I'm the fall guy and maybe I was set up to..."

"...remember, Mr. Denning, that money was to help ransom my husband. Five-thousand dollars."

"Well, now, it seems Berguson needed a little more collateral and upped the ante, kidnapping your sister in the process. Only you didn't count on that, did you, Mrs. Winston?"

Eleanor Winston bristled. I knew I had gotten her goat again, and I was sorry. But I'm like a wolf that goes for the jugular when I'm on the job. "Nothing Leon Berguson perpetrated would surprise me, Mr. Denning. I thought he really knew the whereabouts of my husband and—"

"—he does," Madam Zorrie chimed in. "But it's far more than that. It's bigger than Fredericka's broken heart, the stolen envelope with the money, or even your husband's kidnapping. Hold on...this is going to be a rough ride."

Mrs. Winston glanced at me with fear in her eyes. I knew that look from people who had seen something they shouldn't have but didn't realize they had seen it. Then she turned to Madam Zorrie. "Zorrie, what are we going to do? Where do we begin? Fredericka's safety is still my first concern, no matter what else."

"Eleanor," the gypsy said, trying to console her lovely friend. "You've got to try to see from the top of the hill. We all live in this little box, a reality forced upon us that isn't necessarily true. If all that I am and all that I consider my gifts and those who communicate with me from other dimensions to be...are real and true, then I tell you this: I see things not of this earth that have happened. Not just now, but hundreds and hundreds of times, over and over, century after century. Only they are hushed by the powers that be. All I can say to you and Mr. Denning is what I said before. Leon Berguson is the only link I see right now." Then the tall woman arose to her full height. "Please, forgive me, but I am tired now and must rest." She came over and hugged Eleanor Winston and shook my hand. "Can you see yourselves out?"

"Yeah, thanks, Madam Zorrie," I said, wondering if any of what this woman told us in the past half-hour had any validity. Except I couldn't deny that dream I had of her last night and she knew my birthdate. "Can we be in touch if something else turns up?"

"No, please. I will contact you if there is something I feel is important for you to know. Do I have the way to get in touch, Mr. Denning?" I went over to her desk and wrote down my name and phone number.

"Thank you, Zorrie, I'm so sorry to have distressed you."

The gypsy smiled a weary smile. "It is what I do."

Mrs. Winston and I left Madam Zorrie's parlor like someone had asked us to put the world's most complex puzzle together over night. It was like being sucked down a whirlpool of sparkling lights that didn't hurt, but you knew you were falling deeper and deeper. I needed a drink and suggested as much to Mrs. Winston. We walked out into the dirty sunlight and crossed the street to a bar called *The Firefly*, a joint that had a run-down restaurant next to it. We found a booth in a dark corner. We sat opposite each other, plunking our elbows on the table. She ordered a three o'clock cocktail and I a double whiskey with a water back.

"So tell me, on the level," I began, "can you make heads or tails out of your gypsy's story? Do you think she's on this side of the crystal ball she works with...or the other?'

"Oh, yes. Famous people from all over come to see Zorrie. She is very gifted...and the real thing, Mr. Denning."

"Well, I suppose we're going to be swept up into this thing together, so I think we should dispense with all this formality. Call me *Cable*."

"You mean you will work for me to find Fredericka, Mr. uh, Cable Denning?" she blubbered.

"Yep. Seems the private dick in me can't resist the thought of having my head blown off now and then," I snickered.

"It feels awkward, since I hardly know you, but if you feel okay with it you may call me Eleanor." She quietly reached into her purse for her checkbook. She scribbled out a check and handed it to me. It said, *Pay to the Order of Cable Denning, the sum of FIVE THOUSAND & no/100's DOLLARS.*

I looked over at this gorgeous woman who kept baffling me with her moves. "Are you sure about this?"

"I want you full time," she said in a resolute voice.

"For that kinda dough, lady, ya got me on Sundays!" I examined the check again. "Yeah, Eleanor Winston, consider that I just threw my hat into your ring. Funny how things work out."

She shivered when I said that. "This is *beyond coincidence*! You were chosen for a reason."

"Beyond coincidence? What...now you're going psychic on me like your friend?"

"I think everyone's psychic, Cable. Just in different degrees. I don't believe in coincidences...not really."

"Well, I dunno. It's true sometimes hunches have saved my neck. Like the other night when I was supposed to walk you across the street to your car. My gut put up red lights like a fleet of cop cars. So we turned left."

"See? I knew that about you. I could sense it."

"I even dreamed about your Madam Zorrie the night before—whom you might recollect...I never met until today."

"You what?"

"She was chasing me, pointing one of those long fingers over my head while a maddening ring in my skull kept me running until I finally woke up and picked up the phone."

"This really happened?" she asked, incredulous.

"Ask your friend. She even *knew* she was in my dream. And to top it all off, she knew my birthday was the middle of September."

Eleanor Winston sat back looking at me, studying my face, my eyes, trying to figure me. "You're quite a guy. I never saw you as a soft-touch kind of man. But I see you're quite sensitive inside. That's why I had a fifty-fifty chance of getting you to work for me by sending you that telegram."

"Oh by the way, thanks for that. I usually don't like dames soft-soaping' me, but I knew you meant it. And that you were in trouble. I was out of line unloading my frustrations on you last night."

She smiled at me and I could have taken that babe in my arms then and there and easily forgotten about Fredericka, Madam Zorrie or this strange case I had just jumped into with both feet. "I hope we become friends, Cable," she said. There was wistfulness in her voice few guys could ignore, but I had to keep some kind of guard up. I didn't wanna fall for this dame any more than I already had. And now that she was a client.... full time...

"I'm uh, I'm not too sure of that, Eleanor. This check here in my pocket says that you're my client. Remember what I told you about truth? I kinda like to draw that *truth-line*—that imaginary boundary that keeps guys like me in line and professional. It'd be so easy to go the other way..."

"I understand, Cable. It's best that way, you're right."

Just then the jukebox in the corner came up with a version of "Once in a While", and I saw Eleanor's eyes mist. It was the kind of song that brought memories floating up from places you thought were dead and gone or when you knew something was over and you could never bring it back.

"Hear that song?" she said in a melancholy voice. Then she proceeded to sing some of its lyrics. Had she known what a sucker I was for a beautiful dame and a pretty song, she may not have sealed her fate that afternoon. But it was too late. I wanted to reach across the table, take her hand, and tell her I'd been there. Tell her once upon a time my heart was ripped out by the roots too. But I just looked at that gorgeous face and listened.

Once in a while may you dream of the moments I shared with you,

Moments before we two...drifted apart.

There is a moment in everyone just before you melt into nothingness, the thing inside that makes you remember that love makes this whole damn thing work. But in this beautiful woman recalling the pain that love brought her long ago, there was also the promise of that new moment...the one that was here as close as her breath to my ear.

I think that I could be contented with yesterday's memory, knowing you'll think of me... once in a while.

The booze had gotten to me a bit and I slurred out a compliment, "That was great, Eleanor Winston. Singer Extraordinaire." She thanked me and smiled.

After a while there was a sadness in our conversation. The kind of melancholy that tells a man and a woman they're lying to each other, stalling, when something else should be happening. Something like a kiss in the dark with candlelight, a moonlight walk by the sea when touching hands tells the whole story, or two people looking at each other in a dark bedroom, feeling for each other's lips and bodies. It was as if time was wasting and we weren't doing the things with it we should, obeying what a natural order demanded of us, instincts that reached out and pulled us to each other like magnets in the invisible world Madam Zorrie Robles lived in.

I had had too many double whiskies and they were beginning to wrap around my tongue and play with my speech. I tried to smoke those Lucky Strikes less frequently because I felt somehow it might make Eleanor feel uncomfortable. Finally, I numbed myself enough to tell her I had to go home to sleep.

"Where do we begin tomorrow?" she asked me, her eyes wide in the semi-dark lounge.

"I don't know. I've gotta talk to Boots."

"Boots?"

"Yeah, he's my sidekick...a real old timer...retired sheriff. The kind that rode horses with a posse, wore a six-gun strapped on his hip and chewed tobacco. He's got a lot of wisdom. He'll give us some clues. He always kick-starts me when I begin on a new case that overwhelms my limited talents. He also says I drink too much gin, smoke too many cigarettes and don't have the right kind of dames in my life."

"Is that true?" she asked, laughing.

"Yep, all of it. I'm the kinda guy who doesn't take himself seriously enough to feel worthy of much outside of a client's needs..."

"What about *your needs*?" she asked in that breathy, sexy voice that made me wanna lay her on the bench of the booth right then and there.

"Why are you taunting me, Eleanor?" Finally I had to spill it. Love can be like the feeling that you have to vomit, that you can't hold it in anymore, that urgent feeling when life doesn't have enough time in it to hold back the power of desire. "You know the lyin' game we've been playing for the past hour or so? I know you know it. I can feel it. Wanna know my needs? My needs are to take you up in my arms...not tomorrow or two weeks from now...but tonight, here, right now, and make love to you like you've never known it." I stopped to take a breath. "And then try to forget it because the pain of it will hurt too much, because no matter what two people have, something always goes wrong, some perversity in human sexual nature trips you up." I slowed my voice. "And then you come to a terrible place and this thing wells up in ya and you tell yourself, once you have it, you don't know what to do with it..."

Eleanor Winston's tears came flowing down her cheeks unchecked. She was looking at me through her blurry vision, licking the tears off her lips as they trickled down. "You're right, we've been playing that game of secret desire, haven't we?" she finally said, her voice quavering. "That's been my experience. Give yourself and it all comes flying back in your face. Love is never understood. But do you really believe that is true for *all* people? Are we that damaged as humans that there can never be a genuine falling in love with someone...and staying there?"

I reached for her hand and she yielded. "I don't know, Eleanor Winston. Maybe it's like a little boy's hope that love stays the same, or a man's hope that his balls won't get in the way and overrule his heart. If he's lucky enough to be in touch with his heart. I don't pretend to know the answers." I sniffed from my emotions, the kind that says tears could've come but didn't. "I just had to get it out, clear the air, know where we stood. Remember me, Mr. Truth?"

She grabbed my hand tighter. "I only know what I feel, Cable. I feel things for you. But I have to sort it out. Too much in these two days. My head is swirling..."

I drove her home to a place in the Glendale hills near Forest Lawn. All the way she held onto my right arm and said nothing. As I let her out I had one of those

56

premonitions again, the one that tells you to duck and slide under your car or else you'll be dead in a few seconds. I pulled Eleanor down with me to the pavement just in time to hear a couple of shots ring out and shatter my side window. I shoved her under the car as I grabbed for my .38. Somewhere behind a hedge by her front door I saw some powder smoke rise into the beam from the porch light.

"Cable!" she whispered, trembling as she held on to me.

"Shh…" I cautioned her. "He's there. By your front door. You stay here." She held on to me as long as she could, but she knew I had to go or else we'd be pinned under my little coupe all night. I rolled out and fired point blank at the place in the hedge where I figured the killer was hidden. I heard a groan and I knew I'd made a lucky shot. Quickly I ran up the lawn and dove onto the grass, shooting once more in the same direction. But this time there was only silence. On guard I stood up and approached the hedge near the door. The light from the porch told me a little blood had spilled out of our attacker. I knew he was gone. I went back to get Eleanor. I reached my hand under my car and she grabbed it. I pulled her up. She threw her arms around my body and held it until I could hardly breathe, and then she pushed her lips onto mine and kissed me like there was no tomorrow. And maybe there wasn't, maybe this was it. Maybe the clock was ticking away for us and it was only a matter of the next lucky shot from the gun of a someone neither of us would ever know.

"You can't stay here. We'll try my place," I said.

"Yes." And that was all she could say.

We drove along in silence for a while. She was still clinging to my right arm. Finally I spoke up. "What year is it?"

"Nineteen forty-two."

"How long have we been fighting the Japs?"

"Less than a year."

"How long has FDR been in office?"

"Since 1932 or 33, I believe. Why?"

"Have you noticed anything strange happening to our country...or is it just my silly gut thing?"

"I think we're going to be prosperous. War always makes an industrial country prosperous, Carlton says."

"Do you miss your husband?"

"He's a good man. I married him because he was safe, secure, intelligent and sound of character."

"Sounds like a boy scout to me. Somewhat older than you?'

"That doesn't matter to a sensible woman. It's what you can live with, or what you can't."

"Are you in love with him?'

"No. I haven't been in love since..."

"Since your first real affair, when you were twenty-two, right?" I started flying by the seat of my pants.

"Something like that. But I don't want to talk about it. I'm here now, with you, trying to untangle a mystery that will bring my sister and my husband back safely to me."

"Are you in love with me?"

She drew silent for a moment. "Yes...I think I am, Cable."

All the way to my place she seemed to be content beside me, as if some part of her had always been there.

When we got to my office I went in first to check things out. When the coast was clear, I brought her into my disheveled bedroom. She didn't seem to mind the empty gin bottle or the filled ashtray or a pair of dirty shorts tossed on the floor. I could tell she was exhausted. I gave her a towel and told her she could go ahead and bathe and kidded that I wouldn't peak. She came out in my robe and I knew there was nothing underneath it. I took her hand and sat her on my bed, then excused myself since I had to clean up, too. I must have smelled like a smoky whiskey mill with perspiration as a chaser. When I came back out, she was asleep. I knew she felt safe with me, in my shack, in my presence. And that was enough. I checked all the doors, turned the little light off by the bedside table and climbed in beside her. She stirred only long enough to hold on to my shoulder with her hand and fell asleep again, exhausted. "Cable, I love you." she barely sighed.

Chapter 3

BEYOND COINCIDENCE

It seemed like something was shoveling disconnected sounds into my ear. The thing shouted and grunted, complained and cajoled, and finally I was awake enough to decipher Boots Blake's voice hollering at me from my desk in the office. "Cable! Cable! Cable, where the hell are you?"

Quickly I looked over to see if I had dreamed that beautiful redhead beside me last night. As she stirred at Boot's voice, a look of contentment came over her face, despite the fact that all we did was sleep. How strange it seemed, that the woman I desired so much would sleep next to me on our first night together...without making love!

I took my robe from off the bed and went out into the office. "Shh...Boots...that woman I told you about *did* stay over after all. But don't go away. Let's the three of us have breakfast. I'll go awaken her, if she isn't already by now."

"You lucky son-of-a-bitch...if she's as downright comely as you say she is, then let me stand in line," Boots joked.

"Ha! You *wish*," I said as I went back into the bedroom.

"Cable. There's someone in your office? I'm not dressed." Eleanor said in a very soft voice.

"It's okay. It's Boots. He's the only one with a key beside Ida, my secretary and the cleaning lady. But as you can see, I haven't been able to afford *her* lately. How about us getting dressed and having breakfast with Boots. I told you he will come up with clues for us about Fred and your husband."

"Yes," she said breathily. "I'm looking forward to meeting your friend. I like to meet interesting people." I went into the bathroom with some fresh clothes and threw her my robe.

"I'll be out in a minute," I said. Knowing that a woman needs more time in the bathroom.

When finally we were all collected in the office, I introduced Eleanor to Boots. I knew they would like each other immediately. We crossed the street and walked over to the Franklin Hotel café at Vista del Mar for breakfast.

Boots was laughing. Eleanor tried, but she was too frayed with the events of the past two days to be very jolly. "Well….so, ya sees, this guy was a triple spy, working for this secret organization, the U.S. Government and a millionaire investor who wanted the secrets of them silly Egyptian hieroglyphics."

"So who won?" Eleanor said, sipping on her coffee.

"Nobody. The Egyptian government froze all visits to the damn site an', well, nobody got nothin'."

While Boots was talking, I'd been doing some thinking. How to get Eleanor out of danger and how to spring me into action. How would I trace down Fred to dig out Berguson again to find Carlton Winston? "If it's alright with you two," I finally spoke up after twenty minutes of letting Boots take the floor to brag about some of his adventures in bird-dogging while a young lawman, "I'd like Eleanor to stay with you, Boots. It's only a matter of hours or days when they'll come into my office like a task force, guns cocked."

Boots and Eleanor looked at each other. As rumpled as she was, she still looked great. Her shiny red hair down to her shoulders, those siren blue-green eyes calling to me, an alabaster skin without a flaw. I thought she looked even sexier without much make-up.

"Yep...I've been thinkin' we gotta git her outta your place too...hee! hee! hee! Looks like I get the damsel and you get to beat the pavement, Cable," Boots snickered, enjoying himself more than I'd seen in months. "Didn't I tell ya we needed some excitement in our lives just the other day?' Then he turned to Eleanor. "Hee! hee! I've only got one bed, though, young lady. So, it looks like we'll have to share."

"You take that terrible sofa *you make me* crash on when I flop over at your joint," I said. "Give Eleanor your bedroom and a clean bathroom."

I could see the disappointment in her eyes. "Do I have to? If so, then somebody must go by my place and pick up several changes of clothing for me and some personal things."

"I'll do it," I said. "Boots, give me some of your sleuthing wisdom. We don't have any clues as to where Berguson vanished with Fredericka, Eleanor's sister. Got any ideas?"

The old policeman twisted his smile and looked at me. "Use your head, Cable. The place I'd go to, is where you'd find the most clues...from where the person lived last."

"Berguson's apartment. Where I dug him up originally?"

"Yep...that's where I'd start."

I drove Eleanor and Boots to his house over in Atwater, a cozy little place he had owned since the early 1920's. He had never married, but he had a woman friend for years, Zelma Hightower, whose father was chief of police in some Podunk town outside of Pasadena. She got sick and died in his arms some years back. That's about as close as Boots ever came to an intimate relationship with a woman, except perhaps in the early days of his youth.

Then I went over to Eleanor's fancy home overlooking Forest Lawn. She had given me the key, but I didn't need it. The door was ajar and the blood from the guy I shot last night was still splattered on the walkway behind the hedge. I drew my .38 and entered cautiously. Obviously, whoever "they" were had gotten there ahead of me. But why here? Were they looking for Fredericka or Eleanor? Or something left behind? Or something they wanted? I packed the things on Eleanor's list and shoved them into a suitcase. I went into her bathroom and grabbed a few personal items she had requested. Then I saw it. There on the floor... something had fallen out of a ceiling light that didn't belong. It looked like a thick tinfoil band-aid with a slight golden hue. It also felt like something I'd never felt before. Maybe metal, yet felt like plastic or paper or some other material.

I got a stepladder from the garage and inspected the light well. There was nothing else. I tucked the strip into my pocket and started out when I heard a rustle in another room. I ran in with my gun drawn. No one. The room was obviously a library and had been ransacked.

Everything had been torn apart, books ripped from their shelves, leather seat cushions cut open and the contents strewn about. My gut told me someone was after what I had in my pocket. But why didn't they find it? Maybe they hadn't gotten that far when I entered and cramped their style.

Then I heard a car roar off and hoped that meant the intruders had gone. I got Eleanor's things, locked the house back up and drove over to Boot's place in Atwater. When I told Eleanor about the burglary, she was upset. "I hate that feeling of intrusion! God knows what else they took."

"Prob'ly nothin'. They was lookin' for somethin' else." Boots chimed in.

I reached into my pocket and showed them my new find from the light well. "Ever seen this before?" I asked as I handed it to Eleanor. "I found it in your bathroom. It had fallen out of a light well, the one above the toilet."

"I've never seen it before. I have no idea what it is. It feels like...like a weird material. Not quite metal, but not paper or plastic. Maybe something belonging somewhere else..." Eleanor seemed mystified.

Boots looked it over. "Damnd'est thing I've ever seen. But ya know with the war 'n all, they're probably manufacturing new crap all the time."

"Well, I'm going to take this over to the one person who might give us a clue."

"Zorrie. Can I come?"

"Nope. It's too risky for you out there. I even had to be careful I wasn't followed on my way over." I said good-bye and started out the door when Eleanor followed me to the coupe.

She put her flat hands on my chest, stood up on tip-toe and kissed me. "Did we make love last night?"

"Ya mean you don't remember?" I kidded her.

"Of course, handsome man. But I wanted to. I'm sorry, I was so exhausted and I felt safe…"

"Save it, baby. I understand. There are perfect times for perfect things. You willing to wait our turn?"

She kissed me again and I got this feeling that I was in the company of a goddess and wondered how one man could get so lucky. "Yes," she purred, "When it's right for us. Please, Cable, be safe. When will I see you?"

"I'll call in after I check out Berguson's old apartment. And I have to continue to decoy them away from you. So I'll probably sleep at my place….alone. I'm afraid the only heat I'll be packin' over there will be my .38. I have a hunch I might be getting a visitor." I grabbed her and held her to me as I pressed my lips hard against hers. This time I felt my feet wiggle inside my shoes. What that dame did to me!

It was after 6:00 p.m. as I neared 5th and Olvera. That was good because parking was only fifteen-cents. I walked down Madam Zorrie's stairs and rang the doorbell. But I didn't hear the buzz. I rang again. After a couple of minutes I heard a faint voice call out. "Who…who is it?" a barely audible feminine voice whimpered.

"Zorrie…it's me, Cable Denning …I've gotta see you!"

I heard the buzzer sound and I entered a very dark room. At the far end of the room, I could just barely make out a figure standing. "How about some light in here, huh?" I said.

"No, don't," replied the faint voice of Madam Zorrie's voice. "Please go away, Cable Denning...what do you want?"

"Are you okay, kid? You sound like you're in distress." I knew she wasn't okay and I quickly moved forward toward her and lit a match. There before me and barely standing, was the bruised face of Madam Zorrie. "So they got to you, too? Those bastards. " She started to fall toward me, I grabbed her and helped her into the dimly lit parlor where the crystal ball hung out. " Do I need to get you to a doctor?"

"No. Thank you, Mr. Denning..."

"Cable, call me Cable. It's time to cut the formal crap."

"Is Eleanor alright? After what I saw last night....."

"Yeah, she's okay. Some gun-happy goon took a couple of shots at us as I was taking her home last night. I wounded him but he got away. I had to put Eleanor up at my place. But even that's dangerous now. So I took her to the home of the only guy I trust in the world."

"Good for you. I'm glad. She needed...needed someone..."

"Hey, kid, you're, you're awful weak. What can I get for you?"

She indicated that some hot chicken broth would be good, but I could see as my eyes adjusted to the semi-darkness that her body had also been beat up pretty good. I helped her undress and drew a hot tub for her. That seemed to revive her somewhat. I dozed in a chair for a while. Soon she emerged looking a lot better. "Thank you, Cable. You are a kind man, just as I saw. Good heart. Eleanor loves you, doesn't she?"

"I think so, Zorrie...and I go around with this feeling that I might possibly have real blood pumping through me after all, and right now I could be the luckiest bloke in the world. And I don't carry any light-weight mashed potatoes for this babe, either."

"I'm glad. You two are good for each other." Her voice was still soft and under par. I hated to spring this on her now, but it seemed a lot of people's lives were at stake over this thing. So, I withdrew the strange strip and handed it to her. "What's this?" she asked, cautiously taking the strip of mysterious composition and studying it.

"Your guess is as good as mine. It fell out of a light well in Eleanor's bathroom while I was picking up some personal stuff for her. And it ain't part of the electrical wiring, let me tell ya."

Zorrie held the piece in her left hand and closed her eyes. "Oh...Oh... Fredericka's energy is on it... she touched it. Oh... how can this be? This is made of a material not native to this planet, Cable. Remember what I told you the first time we met? It scares me." She held the strip away from her. "Here, take it back. I can say no more. At least not today." She handed it back to me almost afraid to touch it anymore for fear it would do something dreadful to her.

"I'm sorry to throw this at you just now, Zorrie," I was quite disturbed by Madam Zorrie's declaration. "So, you were on the level with that alien stuff you were talking about last night, weren't you?"

"Remember our truth pact? You and I don't lie, Cable Denning." She closed her eyes again. "I sense Berguson is mixed up in this, along with another man. Then there's Carlton. I never knew what side he was on."

"Yeah," I said. "And I guess those scientist types are probably in high demand just now. I mean with the war and all."

Zorrie winced with pain and bent over. "Oh! My stomach...it hurts, Cable." She felt her gums. "My mouth feels strangely dry and swollen."

"You sure I can't get you to a doctor?" I was persistent, seeing as how this lovely tall woman might have internal injuries as well as the cuts and bruises from her beating.

"No...no...thanks, Cable. Good broth and rest, and I'll heal."

"What'd those goons want from you, did they say?"

"I think they thought I might have what you've just shown me. Obviously, I didn't. Maybe they thought you and Eleanor had given it to me. So they beat me up for good measure, gave me lots of warnings about not squealing about *anything*, including their beastly beatings on women who don't co-operate."

"I'm sorry, kid. One of these nights I'll catch up with them. I'll give 'em an extra bullet for you."

"Sooner or later, Cable, what goes out—comes back around. So what a thousand lifetimes? Remember what I said about all of us being in unity, connected? We are all made of the same star stuff."

"Yeah...and I have heard similar ideas like that before, Zorrie. It's not easy for me to get.

She gave me a faint smile. "It's okay to doubt. Just be open. I still like you the same. We all come home sooner or later."

I was thinking a mile a minute but I had to change the subject. "Question...Zorrie, what exactly does the husband, Carlton Winston, do?"

"First of all, his last name is not Winston...that's Fred and Eleanor's maiden name. They came from the well-heeled Winston family, out of London originally, I understand. *His* name is Dr. Carlton Zelbacher. All I know is what Eleanor told me. He is a scientist and doing top-secret stuff. What's very strange to me is that Berguson shows up and woos Fred right off her feet just before Carlton disappears. Then Berguson disappears. Had it not been for Fred's silly infatuation and need to find him, Eleanor's money and you finally tracking him down, we wouldn't know as much as we know about him now."

"Zorrie, I realize you need to rest. Just one more question. Where do your spirit powers think I should start to look for Berguson to unravel this thing?"

Once again the seated tall woman closed her eyes and ran her fingers over the smooth crystal ball, glowing there in the twilight of the room. "I see a *statue*. Life-sized. Someone is destined to meet you by a statue."

"Statue..." I mused. "That could be anywhere...from Liberty Island to Golden Gate Park in San Francisco. Can you get any closer?"

"Sorry, Cable. I'll let you know if something more exact is revealed to me. Please take care of yourself, and watch over my beautiful Eleanor. Sometimes it seems lovely people like that are just visiting us for a while."

"Don't say things like that!" I growled, a little annoyed. "It's bad enough with all the other crap that's happening in the world....I don't want to think about..."

"I'm sorry, Cable. Just a psychic's musing."

I went over to the tall, handsome woman and hugged her where she sat. "Yes, that's what bothers me. The psychic part. Take care, kid. Do ya need anything?

"I'll be alright, thanks. Cable Denning...good name. I like you. You're a good man. We'll keep in touch."

"I like you too, Zorrie and you're a hell of a woman."

"How would you know that?"

I laughed, " Let's just say I'm psychic."

I said no more and walked out of Madam Zorrie Robles' fortune telling parlor into the night. But before I went street level I peered up and over the sidewalk to make sure no goons were waiting to greet me. The coast was clear.

Needles in the Haystack

Despite Zorrie's prediction about the statue, I still didn't know where to begin looking...except Berguson's old apartment. I also had a bad feeling about Zorrie. I didn't think she'd seen the last of those murderous thugs who were behind this whole crazy unfolding nightmare.

I stopped for a hot dog and a cup of coffee. Across the street, I could swear there was a small man with glasses checking me out, pretending to read a newspaper. Being a private dick, you get a sixth-sense about these things. He didn't quite fit, maybe a European. I decided to engage that eye in the back of my head in case I had to cover my back.

I took the long way to Berguson's dump. I removed the mystery-strip from my pocket and slid it under the floor mat on the passenger side of my coupe. I couldn't take any chances being mugged with that property in my possession. Especially since I still didn't know what the hell it was.

Berguson seemed to favor places with no working electricity, so I fumbled my way around his dingy little apartment with a flashlight. Nothing. I felt disappointed, but then a hot wire went on in my head and I went outside to the garbage cans. It appeared no one had picked them up for weeks. I went rummaging through the kinda shit humans throw away. It was pretty vile. But a crumpled up yellow piece of paper caught my eye. I grabbed it for the hell of it. Who knows?

Bingo! There was a typed note: *...meet Wednesday 4 p.m....FL at David's.....K.* Now who in the hell was 'K', I wondered. Today was Friday. Five days to wait. I knew it was a long shot, but what else did I have? At that moment I was glad I hadn't decided to become a plasterer, because now two and two began to add up. Now all I had to figure out was, what did "*at David's*" mean? I thrust the note into my pocket and cautiously started for the street. There was a green Plymouth coupe parked several cars down from mine that wasn't there before. The streetlight let me see that someone was still inside. I dashed into my car and took off at a normal speed. Soon the headlights of the green Plymouth turned on and the car pulled out into the street. Now I knew for sure. I had picked up a tail.

I went back to my place to call Boots. My office looked like a cyclone had hit it. Papers had been taken out of my private files and strewn on the floor, my bedroom had been torn apart, even my dirty socks and shorts tossed out of the hamper. I grabbed the phone and dialed. "Yeah, it'd better be who I *think* it'd better be," growled Boots.

"Yeah Boots, it's me. I think Berguson's thugs just hit my office without me in it. It's like a rummage sale here. Name it....it's on the floor. Sometimes it's a good thing not to own anything worth a shit. We might as well be taking all this crap off to the dump, including me."

"Sorry to hear that," Boot's comforting old gruff voice said. "You'd better get over here and outta danger, kid. Sounds to me like you're dealing with some pretty tough hombres. And I got a feelin' they're not gonna stop any time soon."

"No can do, Boots. I picked up a tail. I've gotta stay low and be sure I don't make ripples. I don't think they'll be comin' back to my joint...at least not tonight. Who would? Even I don't wanna be here."

"You'd be surprised how criminals think. Remember what I always tol' ya, Cable. Ya gotta think like one to nab one. Hey! Did ya find anything over at Berguson's?"

"Yep. Sure did. I have to hand it to ya, pal; you're a bird dog. But I can't tell you on the phone. I mean, we don't even know if someone might be tappin' the line right now. But...let's do this. Let's meet tomorrow noon at our old meeting place, comprende? And bring Eleanor with a packed bag."

"Well, you tell 'er. She's right here rearin' up and rarin' to talk to ya."

"So put her on..."

"Hello, darling, how are you?" She asked. As soon as I heard her voice my pulse slowed down by fifty beats a minute. Even the dame's voice had a magic effect on me.

She brought me quiet nights by the fire, happy walks by the shores of the ocean and delirious nights wrapped up in each other. "Cable...I miss you."

"I miss you, too, babe. But I got some good news for a change. I'm sorry you've been cooped up with the ol' cowboy."

"I like that old cowboy," she laughed. "He's one of the best storytellers I've ever heard." I could hear Boots bitch in the background.

"Ha! Okay then. So, guess what? You and I are going somewhere special for a couple of days. Just pack a few things. Boots knows where to rendezvous. I can't wait to get my arms around you and show you how strong my muscles have gotten since I held you last."

She was excited and laughed. "That was this morning, silly."

I didn't know how to break the news about Zorrie's beating. But I knew they were good friends and she would comfort the gypsy. " Um, I think you should call Zorrie. She's not feelin' so hot. Seems some of Berguson's tough guys roughed her up a bit, looking for something."

"Oh, no, Cable! Is she badly hurt?"

"Well, doll, she's in pain, a few cuts and bruises. I offered to take her to a doc, but she felt chicken soup and rest would do the trick."

"That's Zorrie. Oh, dear I will call her immediately."

"Until tomorrow noon, Eleanor Winston. Put Boots back on the phone, will ya?"

"Good-night, sweetheart. Until tomorrow. I'm excited, Cable. Please, I beg you, stay safe and take no chances, private investigator or not, I want all of you with me in one piece."

Boots came back on the phone. "Yeah?" Boots growled.

"These guys are starting to play hard ball, Boots, and I don't know what inning we're in. We gotta lay low until we know what's really going on here. I think it's a lot bigger than we figured."

"Well, looks like we got that excitement I was tellin' you about, eh? Son of a bitch, Cable, and you and me are the only posse. I hope the hell we can hold 'em off at the pass."

"Yeah, looks like the whole damn thing is comin' in like a loaded freight train. We gotta watch our backs from all angles. See ya tomorrow." I hung up and looked around at the disaster that used to be my office. It never was what you might call orderly, but it worked and I knew where everything was. Maybe I should toss it all out and start over again. You know, the old saying, *new woman, new clothes, new house, new life*? Actually, I just made it up, but it sounds good, somehow. I noticed that since I'd known my little goddess, I smoked and drank less than I had in years. And for Cable Denning, that was an accomplishment.

I gathered up my stuff from off of the floor in the bedroom, scrambled a few blankets together with my pillow and my bed was ready. I smoked my last cigarette and took a small shot of gin. On my way to bed I tripped over my box-radio. It seemed undamaged, so I put it back up on my dresser and turned it on. Maybe some nice big band music would relax me. Whether it was fate or coincidence, the radio station I usually listen to had been knocked off its tuning point on the dial. So instead it had this crazy colored preacher on a Negro radio station, energetically spewing out a bunch of crap. Or was it? Then he said something that stopped my tired brain in its tracks.

"This war we have entered into is not for the people. No war is for the people. We stole the Hawaiian Islands from the Hawaiians. We had no business placin' military bases and warship harbors in its beautiful waters. We are not defending our country three thousand miles away. We are defending our financial interests. War is for the moneymakers to make more money. No less a man of stature than the honored Thomas Jefferson said, "I sincerely believe...that banking establishments are more dangerous than standing armies." End quote. What do you say, my faithful of the Lord? What do you say about this? Does the Lord's providence care more about the rich man than the poor? Not in my Good Book, it don't! Nor in our Good Book is there any reference to the rich getting richer at the expense of us poor who are unknown and unrecognized in this world.

It is true that we have been attacked by an unconscionable enemy. The Japanese have slain our Goliath in the Hawaiian Islands. But no matter what happens outside our borders, we remainin' here have a voice, a place—and unless our rights as black people are recognized as equal to any white man's, we shall go down in history as mock-slaves living a pretense of freedom!"

This guy hit me where I live. Something in his voice was not only sincere, but somehow he wasn't speaking just for the Negroes of America, but for the common man. He was looking for truth, my kind of truth—for all people. Either we had equality or we didn't. So far we didn't. Then there was a pause and the announcer said I was listening to Reverend Jerome Malmouth of Heaven's Glory Baptist Church in Los Angeles. I had to hear more. I glued my ear to the radio.

"At a time like this, we know it was difficult for our president to make the decision he did last December. We know he must answer not only to his constituents, the law of the land and the new circumstances that engulf our nation, but he must answer to GOD. No man exchanges his Adamic soul for his celestial place in Heaven without that accountability. Now, I know many of you do not know this. But for some months our president has been working on a SECOND BILL OF RIGHTS. Why is this so? Because Mr. Roosevelt sees the inequity between the haves and the have-nots! Hallelujah! None of God's children should fall subject to favoritism or bias! This Roosevelt proposes the most fair-sweepin' entitlement this country has ever known!" The congregation applauded enthusiastically.

"What does this mean? He has been constructing a house. He has been building a dream for all of us. Allow us to see this, O Lord, as inspired of You, and not the man who proposes it. These are the words which must turn into glorious reality: A JOB, ADEQUATE WAGES FOR A DAY'S WORK WELL DONE, A DECENT HOME TO LIVE IN, MEDICAL CARE WE CAN AFFORD, ECONOMIC PROTECTION DURING SICKNESS, ACCIDENT OR OLD AGE— and last, but surely not least, A GOOD EDUCATION FOR ALL." Again the radio sounded with applause and enthusiastic 'Hallelujahs' and 'Amens'.

The Reverend paused. He hummed *Amazing Grace* for a moment. Then this wonderful female gospel singer started up singin' like the angels were comin' to get her. The congregation was yellin' and screamin' throughout the whole song....they were having a great time! Finally the minister continued.

"On this Friday night in the City of Angels...the devil... the devil, I say, in the form of sin, is having a holiday. Satan dances on or off the battlefield. Bordellos are full, bars are full, dance halls are full and other dens of iniquity flourish while mankind dwells on in darkness and ignorance." But as he went on, the Reverend now shocked me.

"Congress.....is filled with criminals.......and thus the very rich. Even this President, with his noble words, his honorable intentions and perhaps an honest heart, like all presidents...is a criminal...selling out to the rich. The Supreme Court is filled with violators of Holy Law, who are bought and paid for by private industry. The military is criminal, for in saying yes to kill another human being, they are perpetuating a sin against the Lord!

What other secrets lie hidden behind locked doors in scientific laboratories creatin' weapons to control a people just as we are controlled by a government who since Abraham Lincoln has promised us equity and prosperity.....and has yet to deliver!" Again shouts and yells with clapping and praising God and all the usual. The choir began to sing.

I changed the radio station 'til I heard some sexy young singer. Even though I was exhausted, the Reverend Malmouth's words echoed in my brain. It was kinda like the jam I was in. Who knew what powers controlled what was happening? What if that strange little strip I had in my possession had been manufactured by secret labs? Of course, I thought, it could also all be part of a big nothing. I fell asleep tossing and turning, still seeing poor Zorrie's beat up face and hearing her beaten-down voice. How quickly one moment can change our lives. But I was also fantasizing about Eleanor and what I'd do with her when we got to Santa Barbara. I was going to take her to the El Encanto, on top of the hill over-looking the town and the ocean. Well, let me tell ya...a couple of nights in one of their private bungalows with that doll would cure any man of what ailed him. With *that* kind of smile on my face, I finally drifted off into a more or less peaceful sleep.

Chapter 4

THE KNIFE THAT TWISTS

Deep inside I was delirious with pain. I was heart-sick. When a tough guy like me falls for a classy babe like Eleanor Winston, all stops get kicked out. Suddenly you find yourself in free-fall, like nothing else matters more than the object of your affection. Even though it's entrenched deep down, there's just something that keeps nagging you to stay in control...so you keep running. You run from all the things you tried and failed to be in life—you run from the humdrum of everyday existence—you run from the cruelty and senselessness of the world and you find yourself separated out because you don't understand the human race. But what was I running *to*?

How do you figure a dame like her, hooked-up with a loser like me, a second-rate, down and out private dick, working for nickels and dimes to pay the bills, buy bullets and put gin, cigarettes and a little food on the table. What could she possibly see in my mug that attracted her? Maybe it was the mother in her seeing the quiet desperation that haunted my waking hours—the frozen kind, like when you're a little boy and something bad gets branded into your brain and from that day on it shows up in your eyes. Maybe that's what she saw.

As we buzzed up the Pacific Coast Highway toward Ventura, I could feel her happiness. For years I'd been alone, so self-absorbed. At the same time, my job kept my nose in everyone else's problems but mine. To know that me just being around makes someone else feel really good for all the right reasons sat just fine at the bottom of my gut. It was like I was becoming part of her, and if she loved me like I thought she might, the same was happening to her. "Oh, Cable, I can't believe it. It's all happened so fast...everything."

"Yeah, it's like life tosses you up on a merry-go-round ride. But you know, babe, I think I've been waiting for you my whole life.

She hunkered down in her part of the car seat and smiled with wonderment like a little girl. "Have you? Oh....Cable. So where are you taking me?"

"Surprise."

"I do like surprises. I love Santa Barbara. Years ago my folks lived there, up on Cliff Drive."

"You never talk about your parents. Are they alive?"

"No," she said with a peculiar sadness in her voice. "They died in a plane crash in 1937."

"I'm sorry." I patted her leg. "Were you close?"

"Yes. I adored my parents. They were handsome, intelligent, kind and beautiful people and I miss them..."

"Like you, babe." She snuggled up to me and kissed my shoulder. "Eleanor, it's been on my mind...what do you see in a guy like me? I sure ain't one of your Hollywood types. Especially after the rough start we had. I wouldn't have blamed you for walkin' right out on me the way I treated you that first night."

"The heart is funny, Cable," she said with a very serious voice. "We never know who we'll end up with, why we end up with them, or how long something will last." She paused. "I don't *know* what attracts people to each other. Kids, young people are another story. When we're very young, we're so full of youth and vitality...romance and sex become the objective....didn't it you?"

"Nope. I was too busy keeping hoodlums offa my front porch so my mother could hang her wash. Far as I can figure, all we got is today. After that, you can lay all the odds you wanna...but it's anybody's guess."

Then her face grew taut. "I am still worried about Fred...what if...what if—?"

"—Find Berguson and we'll find your sister."

"Oh, Cable, I hope you're right."

"I've been in this business a long time. I'll wager Berguson took off with your sister to hedge his own bets. He's a lot of shitty things but I don't think he's a killer. Plus, if she still has a yen for him, he'll use her charms to take care of his other needs. I know how these guys operate."

"What terrible people there are in the world!"

"Yeah, and what's worse, ya never know who they are. Some of the worst criminals are people in power. Look at Yamaguchi or whoever the hell that Jap admiral is, or the fancy party Hitler's throwing for his pals in Europe. These guys make Genghis Khan look like a warm-up act for a comedy show."

She was fidgeting with her hair...you know, like women do... twirling strands around a finger while in thought. "Everything is so unsettled."

I laughed "Welcome to life, babe. The name of the game is to keep us off balance. But so what? We've got today....just say you'll be with me *now*. I won't even ask you for tomorrow unless you wanna be there."

She held my arm tight. Then she pulled up and kissed my five-o'clock shadow. "I *am* with you, Cable. I may not know all the answers, but I'm here...with Cable Denning, private eye, master detective."

"Well, that part remains to be seen. Hang on to your hat, this thing ain't over yet."

She began to have that daydreaming look. "Have you ever been to Italy?"

"Oh yeah....I've been to Italy...but, if you don't mind, that's a whole other story. Why do you ask?"

"Oh....well, I was just thinking about Florence. It was so lovely. I remember I went with my parents and my Uncle Chit...short for Chitchester. The main Duomo is gigantic, but most of all, I remember being awe-struck by Michelangelo's fourteen foot statue of *David*...it was so magni—"

"—*David!* That's it! You're a genius, Eleanor Winston!" I pulled to the side of the road, grabbed her and gave her a great big smack right on those luscious lips...hard. "Berguson's note—'*Meet 4 p.m....FL...at David's*'. Don't you see? It's the statue! There's a famous one at Forest Lawn....and that's the *FL!*...of course!" '*Meet 4 pm.....Forest Lawn at David's statue*'!"

"Oh, that's wonderful! Now we can start to find Fred—and Carlton."

Parked by the side of the road and feeling the whoosh of traffic flying by us, I suddenly realized something. "Carlton. He's your husband. You're going off with me. Does that feel right with you? Or should we have discussed this before?"

Eleanor took my arm and gently patted it as she looked into my eyes with those blue-green lamps of

82

hers. "We haven't had a true marriage in years, Cable. It's been in name only. I guess I was marrying my father. Kind, intelligent, capable, on the cutting edge of new technologies—that's Carlton. But I forgot I was a woman and I loved to be touched. Carlton didn't know how." She brought her lips very close to mine. "I can't wait until that moment when the door clicks shut behind us and we're alone together, finally."

That was some pretty bold talk for a dame who was used to party manners and society dances. But I had already jumped in with both feet. And ya know?—I didn't wanna get out, leave, run, escape, have a fling and then forget the dame a week or so later. No, not this time. This time I wanted to stay. "Yeah me, too. You'll find that after a few minutes alone, we're gonna run outta words. And all we'll have left to do is this..." I kissed her on those moist, welcoming lips and again was transported right out of this crazy world.

"Is that a promise?" she whispered to me.

"You bet."

We arrived at the El Encanto about four o'clock. Eleanor's eyes were full of memories. She had toddled the gardens and walkways with hanging vines and flowers when she was a young child. "I remember my mother and father, sitting in the lounge having a glass of Champagne and letting me have a tiny sip."

I left Eleanor in the car. I entered the sedate lobby and approached the desk. But I wish I hadn't...I wish I'd been more careful. Standing over by a newsstand not far away, was a man pretending to read a paper. But he was watching my every move. I checked in and decided not to tell Eleanor. When I got back in the car, I shot her a smile and tried to get back into the same mood I had when I left her. "We gotta drive to the other side of that walkway and find an assigned parking space."

We gathered our few belongings and turned to find our place. I was keeping my eyes open, checking all the hidden corners...but this time Eleanor's instincts picked it up. "We're being watched, aren't we? Someone's here." she said without missing a beat.

"Yeah. Don't look back over your shoulder. Let me unlock the door. We'll enter and go in, as if we haven't noticed anything."

We made our way to Bungalow #4. We tried to make it as natural as possible. I twisted the key in the lock, opened the door and gently pushed Eleanor in. Then I locked and chained the door. We both took a deep breath.

I smiled at this beautiful woman who was standing in front of me. "Well, don't look now, lady, but you're alone with a strange man," I quipped.

"Yes. A strange man I like," she whispered softly.

"I've got a small bottle of gin here, in case we need a bit of fortifying."

Eleanor excused herself and went into the bathroom. The bungalow was old; it had a smell of the damp sea air from the nearby ocean. An old radio sat on a dresser along with a couple of art deco lamps. I turned on some nice background music. Soon my voluptuous redhead returned stripped down to her slip. "See anything you like, big boy?" she teased.

"I like the whole package, doll. That almost see-through brassiere of yours doesn't make it easy to keep my hands off you."

She approached with the two glasses sitting on a side table. "So who said to keep your hands off?" I poured some gin in our glasses and we toasted. "After all, Mr. Denning, when this woman says *yes*, she means it."

"Well, here's to us." I said, as I gulped every drop of my gin down.

We sat on the bed and made overtures like a conductor warming up his orchestra for the big symphony. I still couldn't believe my luck. Of all the dames in the world, this one walked into my office. There's something about a woman who seems to be prim and proper in her working hours and then turns into a warm, seductive siren when the lights go down. She reached for me and undid my tie. "This has to come off." Then she began to unbutton my shirt. "And this, too." I reached over to the nightstand and turned the light off. A dim glow from a street lamp in the parking area filtered through the drapes as I watched her take her clothes off. I didn't waste any time, either.

Soon we had slipped under the sheets together, my lips forcing her head into the pillow. Feeling my body connect with hers stem to stern sent my heart rate over the top. She began to purr and moan as I mounted her and my hand slipped up between her legs. "Oh, Cable..." She whimpered with pleasure for a second and then pulled me into her. Eleanor was a *woman* in every possible sense of the word.

We spent the whole night making one kind of love or another. Sometimes it was just looking at each other with those child-like expressions of delight. Other moments she was licking the juices that had intermingled as a result of our erotic passion. "I don't want to waste a drop of you...I want every bit of you inside me!" she had whispered in one particularly ecstatic moment. I noticed the booze and the cigarettes had slowed me down through the years, since Eleanor was probably ten years my junior. But what the hell, I figured, what better way to get in shape?

Late the next morning we sat in the El Encanto coffee shop, sipping a hot, black brew. I got the distinct feeling others were watching us. In fact, they were. We must have appeared like two honeymooners on the lamb.

"What do you want to do today?" She asked me.

"Go back to bed with you."

She laughed quietly and raised her eyebrow in approval. "Well, we *can* do that...or we can take a nice walk along Hendry's Beach at the end of Las Positas Drive."

"Okay," I laughed. "How about both?'

And that's exactly what we did. Every time I got near her I could smell me on her and that excited me. It was like she was oozing my essence out of her pores.

On the way back from a long, leisurely walk on the beach, we were heading back to the hotel when she asked something peculiar. "Do you know what I'd like to do with you? Like a teenager, take in a movie at the Arlington Theater."

"Why not?" I laughed. "The whole day is ours, babe."

My interests did not usually go the way of the motion picture attending public. I already had more than my share of drama in my life. Why in the hell would I want to see a Hollywood version of it? But for Eleanor I would have climbed the Empire State Building in telephone-pole cleats.

The Arlington was one of the nation's premiere theatres. I'd heard of its incredible size and unique decor. When we entered, the lights were just high enough between movies so people wouldn't trip in the aisles. But what was unique to this showplace of the 1930's was that they had built what looked like an entire Mexican village inside the damn place! The sides had those quaint little haciendas, lit up from the inside, looking like a welcome wagon for the distraught traveler. The huge domed ceiling was a warm, starry Mexican night. Wow!

Eleanor knew the theatre well and had spent many an hour in her younger years watching Norma Shearer, Bette Davis, Joan Crawford, Clark Gable, Edward G. Robinson, George Raft, Laurel and Hardy and that whole parade of movie stars Hollywood had created to keep 'em comin'. But she really loved musicals. She said she had thrilled to Jeanette MacDonald and Nelson Eddy in a particular movie I had never seen, entitled *Maytime*. So guess what was playing for the matinee performance? Yep—she told me it was making its second go 'round from its original 1937 release,.

The movie started and there in the dark we held hands tightly like desperate teenagers, afraid of losing this moment when we'd have to leave and go home to our parents. But something about the newsreel caught my attention. There was an aerial view of a farmer's crop-field somewhere in England. What was eerie about the whole thing was, that the announcer suggested that the perfect geometrical patterns in the grain stalks below could not have been made by human tools...at least, not from the ground. A local meteorologist was interviewed and suggested it was the result of unidentified spacecraft seen buzzing around that part of the English sky lately. Saucer-like discs, darting here and there.

Eleanor and I looked at each other. She was smiling. Somehow this seemed different than having real experiences with other-dimensional beings. These strange vehicles darting about leaving mysterious markings below in the fields...I don't know...something about it...the whole thing gave me the shivers.

But, actually, I enjoyed the main feature. I wasn't particularly a fan of high-brow music, but when that dish MacDonald, was shown from the time she was an old voice teacher, to flashbacks to her earlier luminous singing career, rather caught me in the craw. She turned me on. Maybe it was because Eleanor had turned up my thermostat so high that any dish with good looks and charm could catch my pants on fire. Eddy was a bit stiff, but by the time Barrymore had killed him out of jealousy, I was on his side.

Just as the film ended and the lights came up, I could swear I saw a man in a dark coat and hat peering down at us from one of those Mexican haciendas above. I grabbed Eleanor's hand and led her to the safety of the crowded lobby. "What is it, Cable?", she asked. I told her to stay put and I raced down a small flight of stairs, which I figured led to the interiors of the little Mexican village. I was right. Just as I started up to rooms above, I saw a figure coming down toward me. But he saw me and reversed his direction, but before he did, I saw the glint of a gun in the semi-light as he hid behind a wall. I drew my .38.

"Is that you, Berguson?"

"Yeah, what of it?"

"You'd make a lousy detective. What the hell do you want...and where's Fredericka?"

"I'm protecting my investment, on all counts. You've got something I want, Denning. And Fred's alive...for now. But she won't be for long, if you don't hand over what you've got."

I didn't even know what I had, so I pushed him. "And what might that be, Berguson?"

"The *electra*-strip you found at Fred and Eleanor's place. Carlton hid it there but never told Fred. But it's useless without a companion-piece. Hand it over, Denning, and I won't kill you."

"Come and get it, Berguson. You seem to be the wise guy with all the answers."

But he didn't call my bluff. "Another time, another place. I'm leaving now. But I won't be taking my eyes off you until I've got the strip. And don't think Eleanor's safe, because she ain't. I'll stop at nothing to get that strip. Got it, Denning?"

"Yeah, I got it, Berguson." But I wasn't gonna let him get away that easy. I lunged forward, rolling on the floor toward the direction of Berguson's voice. But he saw me and darted as quick as a jack-fly down some stairs leading to the rear exit of the theatre. By the time I got there he was gone.

I ran out of the little casa back out into the lobby. A worried look played across Eleanor's lovely face. "Cable...who was it?"

"Who else...Berguson. Let's go." On the way back to the El Encanto I informed her that Berguson said that Fredericka was all right. Probably a bit shaken realizing that she had been kidnapped by her ex-lover. I also told her that Berguson had called our mystery object an *electra*-strip, that there was a companion piece to it...and nothing would stop this madman from obtaining it. But who was *he* working for? I knew in my gut he wasn't that sharp to be running the whole operation alone. I figured him an expendable fall guy who would sooner or later take the rap.

"We can't stay then...can we?" Eleanor asked, with a tear in her voice like a young woman suddenly deprived of her honeymoon.

"No babe. We gotta scram and get back to L.A. I'm gonna gather up Boots and flush this rat out of his hole. Sorry, honey, will ya take a rain check?"

She took my arm and rested her head on it. "Only if you'll be there...I mean all of you."

"Soon as this thing blows over, babe, we're gonna do something we've never done before. We're gonna take a cruise to Mexico...ever been? And ya don't get seasick, do ya?"

"Oh, Cable, yes! And no....I don't get seasick.

Chapter 5

THE TERRIBLE MR. X

Gabriel Heatter was on KHJ radio as we drove back. He always had this slick, nefarious sounding voice, the kind that belonged to the villain in some tawdry Saturday matinee about the treasures of Mai Ling and the taking over of America by subversive Asian powers. But today he was saying something that got my attention.

"Now, on the odd side of the news. It seems, citizens of this land, some time ago when I told you about the retrieval of a military aircraft near the town of Cape Girardeau, Missouri, last April—it was reported at that time not only all aboard had perished, but other very bizarre and certainly erroneous rumors abounded by the local folk. For example, that aircraft was not military but private in origin—and might have been an experimental craft of some sort. As you know, our wartime military efforts must surely result in the design and construction of top-secret craft to protect this great country of ours. We cannot, nor shall we, forget the plight of Los Angeles on the night of last February 24th, when most likely our most advanced system of testing our readiness for Japanese invasion was launched into Los Angeles skies.

On a last curious word, however, getting back to the bizarre events near Cape Girardeau, the reputable local sheriff, one Ruben Reinhold Schade, is quoted as saying he is still dealing with a disturbed local populace and has spoken with, quote "very frightened and somewhat intimidated townsfolk who swore they had seen a spaceship with little people aboard". End quote. What isolated country folk won't do for a modicum of publicity, eh?

In other news, it seems Chancellor-turned-dictator Hitler of Germany considers the Japanese invasion a natural reaction as the Allies have invaded a land that was never theirs but oriental by origin. Until next time, America.

I clicked the radio off. I was thinking. Why would Heatter be bringing an old buried news story back up now? For public interest? "Did that sound odd to you?" I asked Eleanor.

"No, why, should it? The scare we all had last month stays with people for a while. Perhaps it's not odd that other such events are occurring all over the world. Who knows?"

"I don't know. It had a funny ring to it. You know me and my sixth sense. That gut feeling."

"My busy-brained darling, sometimes it's more of a burden than a blessing, isn't it?"

"Something like that." Then I changed the subject. I had this nagging feeling all day. "I think we'd better check on Zorrie Robles."

By the time we arrived back in LA my gut was doing flip-flops. We drove right to Zorrie Robles' place. We rang the bell and pounded on the gypsy's front door to no avail. Finally, we got the building superintendent to let us in. But it was too late. Madam Zorrie Robles was dead. Sometime within the past forty-eight hours she had been strangled. She laid there on her sofa bed her eyes staring up to the stars that she was so connected to. I was sorry because I liked her, because she was still young and beautiful in her own way, and because she was Eleanor's friend. And Eleanor—she was busted up pretty good. Zorrie Robles was that soul sister women have in their lives if they're lucky enough to find them. I took Eleanor in my arms and held her in the outside parlor while she wept on my shoulder.

"I loved her so much. We were so close in so many ways. She even saw you coming into my life months ago. Oh, Cable, how can we stop this terrible thing that's happening to all of us?"

"I dunno, Eleanor. How do you stop a war? Gangsters are like vermin that crawl out of the darkness and kill without conscience. Like Hitler's krauts. It doesn't matter who or how many you do-in to achieve the goal."

Then Eleanor clung to me even tighter. "Thank God for you in my life, darling I would be lost without you right now, Cable."

I kissed her and sat her on the sofa in the waiting room. I went back to look at Zorrie's body. In a strange way death became her. So if one's gottta go, perhaps it was an appropriate thing that she would be staring up at those mysterious stars she counted on to deliver those mystical communiqués her customers counted on. Like life, who could figure the craziness of it all?

"Now the cops would have to be involved. I phoned Lester Keith, a cop I trusted and knew for many years. As usual, he wasn't happy to hear from me.

"So ya gotta stiff, eh Denning? Who is it this time…a jealous husband snuffing out his wife…or girlfriend?"

"Nope, not this time. I think it's a case of the girl who knew too much. Just plain ol' fashioned criminal violence."

"No crime of passion? Not as exciting for you, eh? How'd she get it?"

"Beating...then strangulation. I don't think you'd say this case was without passion, Lieutenant, just not the kind you mean. It kinda grows like a balloon you're blowing up, but you can't stop it from getting bigger and...Bam!"

"My, my, Denning. Sounds like you're a bit ragged around the edges. I'll come out and poke around and even bring a nice clean wagon from the morgue to pick up the victim, free delivery. Then I'll need a lot of information...from you."

Eleanor sat in the outer room, still distraught. "Poor Zorrie...she never bothered anyone. She was very good at what she did." Then she steeled herself. "I suppose this is Berguson's work? I never could stand him. Now I hate him, if he did this."

I put my arm around her as I sat next to her. "Yeah, that makes two of us, kid. But...I'm not sure, babe. I don't see it as Berguson's style. I said before that I don't see him as a killer. But I could be wrong."

When Lt. Keith arrived, he pumped us both for answers we didn't have. I filled him in on most of what I knew. Zorrie's first meeting with us, how she saw dark things coming our way. I did leave out one detail, however...about the *electra*-strip. I thought I would keep that quiet for the time being. He excused us and I took Eleanor back over to Boots' place.

"Whatsa matter, fellow travelers? Back already? The little woman dished out more than you could handle, eh?" Boots quipped as he answered the door and saw both of us standing there.

"They killed Zorrie Robles, Boots," Eleanor cried as she entered and hugged the old man with the cranky growl.

"Awww, no..." Then he looked up at me. "It ain't Berguson, is it? You know, I've been puttin' a lotta things together while you two were romancin' at the sea in Santa Barbara." He helped Eleanor sit down on the sofa and took a chair directly across. I stayed standing, kinda misplaced, thinking about where *I* would spend the night. "You're not sayin' anythin', Cable...cat got your tongue?"

I told Boots about the encounter with Berguson in Santa Barbara at the theatre. I decided to tell him the stuff about the *electra*-strip, but the old fox didn't blink an eye.

"Did ya happen to catch that Gabriel Heatter on the radio today by any chance?" He asked.

"Why, yes, we did," Eleanor said, raising her eyebrows. Cable's interest seemed piqued by it, but I thought it was just a broadcast hype."

"Well, there's your answer, Mr. Private Investigator," Boots bragged, his voice sounded gruff and important.

But I didn't get it. What in the hell was that ruffian old man saying? "What answer, Boots? Don't yank me around just now, I'm too tired from trying to figure this whole damn merry-go-round." But the old man remained adamant. "That's the whole answer, Cable...that weird 'strip' of yours ain't what ya might call from the— the *local neighborhood*."

"So what...Europe? China? South America?"

Boots went silent. Then slowly he turned his eyes up to the ceiling and held them there. "Try a little less local than that."

When I got his gist I thought...Boots?...never thought I'd see the day. "You mean you're buyin' into the little green men those townspeople were conjuring up to get publicity for Cape Girardeau? Why, Boots! Never figured you for a believer—"

"—I think he's on to something," Eleanor interrupted. "Please, Cable, didn't Zorrie tell us it was alien or something? Please sit down. You're making me nervous pacing the floor. It's been an exasperating day for all of us. Let's have a drink and hear Boots out."

I poured and they sat. Once we had taken a few slugs each, Boots cleared his throat and began to speak. " Well, you know me, Cable, I ain't one to buy into the horse pucky most people wanna sell ya. But I called the local newspaper in Cape Girardeau. Nobody knew anything. The Feds and military that were there, shut everybody up. I guess mum's the word on that strange incident. So, I called an old colleague of mine, Jeremiah Hampson, who just happens to live nearby. Being a retired cop with a good sniffer, I pressed him. And this is a God-fearin' man who ain't too likely to buy into fairy-tales now, I tell ya." Boots took another stiff swallow. "Here's what I found out. Seems a straight-laced Evangelist preacher named Reverend William Huffman got called out of bed about 9:30pm sometime in the spring of last year, to give final rites to some folks who were killed in a small craft crash about fifteen miles outta town. They drive him out and find the location already hummin' with local reporters, cops, and mysterious black cars with no letterin' on 'em. Well now, at the scene, Huffman meets an acquaintance, one Garland Fronabarger, who was one of the first to arrive at the crash site. Fronabarger is a local free-lance photographer. Immediately he informs Huffman that the aircraft was not your typical one-engine, two winged Piper Cub. In fact, it had no visible motors and no wings! An' ta top it off, there were three bodies that were little smooth-skinned creatures with huge eyes, a kinda silvery gray in color an' lookin' very dead. He managed to get a photograph of one before the military came and took charge."

It sounded like great material for one of those Science Fiction magazines. I chuckled, "Whatta ya been drinkin', Boots?" But the truth was, I've learned over the years that sometimes truth can be stranger than fiction.

Eleanor interrupted. "Cable, let him finish. It gives me the shivers, but I—"

"—Yeah, who's tellin' this story? You or me?" Boots interjected. "Keep shut or I'll box your ears back." I went silent and sat down next to Eleanor.

"Now, for safe keepin', Fronabarger passes off the exposed film roll to Huffman just as official types approached to foreswear them to keep shut. This incident never happened. Never. No how. But the Feds don't search the minister and he's told to go home. No word of this must be spoken to *anyone*, they are warned. They do, however, confiscate Fronabarger's camera and he tells them he left in a hurry with no film in the camera. Heh! Heh! The next day the preacher gives Fronabarger back his film and the photographer develops it. He gives one copy of the photograph to Huffman and keeps one for himself. Now the Feds buy the original story and don't follow up."

Eleanor and I sat transfixed as Boots unfolded this preposterous story. But I noticed she was shaking her head in the affirmative while I was nervously puffing on a cigarette.

"So, my old friend Jeremiah, he goes to see this Fronabarger a few days later, you know, after the newspaper spills a short article on the local air crash. Fronabarger knows Jeremiah as a trusted soul. So he shows him the photograph...that he developed in secret...and lo and behold, bam! There it is! The alien lookin' creature underneath the light of a flashbulb!" Boots looked at both of us. I was squinting from the smoke in my eyes, but Eleanor was all ears and looked bright as a penny as her eyes grew wider and wider.

Boots continued. "An' lookin' very unlike a local Cessna, the aircraft turns out to be a round disc about, oh, twenty-feet across. When the rightly Reverend glances inside the broke open hole of the craft, he sees strange gauges and dials and all around the inside were symbols that resembled *Egyptian hieroglyphics*."

I put my smoke out in the ashtray. "Okay, so it's a great story, Boots. If it were true, that might explain our so-called *electra*-strip. Where'd the photographs end up?"

"As I told ya..."Boots suddenly yelled at me, "Aren't ya listenin', boy? Jeremiah says to me each man has one copy. They're hidden away."

My sleuthing little Eleanor added, "Understandably, they're afraid to go to the authorities. God knows what the government would do, especially during wartime.". "

Don't you think it's *possible* this is true?" I shrugged my shoulders but kept quiet.

"It wouldn't matter no how, anyway. The government forced the newspaper to print a 'correction,' that a common, everyday version of a small craft crashed and all were killed. But the next of kin were never notified. Don't ya find that strange?" Boots let out a cackle. "Seems like you'd hafta telegraph an awful long way to reach *those* creatures' folks, eh?" He took another drink. "And that was that. But...the frightened townsfolk who had seen the crash site were each visited by someone from a secret agency and told *'this didn't happen, ya didn't see it, this is national security and it's never to be talked about again.'* Boots took in a deep breath and exhaled toward me. "So what does it sound like to you, Cable?"

"Even a photo can be doctored, Boots," I said, playing the devil's advocate.

"Oh, Cable, for goodness sake. Be open," said Eleanor. "Do you honestly think we're the only creatures living in this vast universe of ours? Even Carlton often spoke of the infinite magnitude of the cosmos. Aren't we being a little myopic to think we are alone amongst billions of stars?" Eleanor insisted.

"I happen to know firsthand that we are not. But we won't go into that now. By the way, dearest Eleanor, I haven't heard your Carlton's name mentioned much lately. Is your concern for him waning? Or is it the blood-thicker-than-water thing, where Fredericka gets priority?"

Something was eating at me and poor Eleanor teared up and she clenched her fist in anger. "Cable!

99

How can you?! I thought we agreed that when I went away with you as a married woman—"

"—I'm sorry," I apologized. "I was out of line, Eleanor. We're all too damn keyed up and tired, I guess. Where in the hell am I gonna sleep, Boots? I can't go back to my place and more than likely Berguson...or whoever...will find your place sooner or later. As I see it, we got three major ends to tie up. One, we get Fred and Carlton back safe and sound...two, we find the other part to this strip...and three, find out who's really behind this dangerous game someone's makin' us play."

With a meek but emotional voice, Eleanor looked at me. "You can sleep with me. The bed's small. I hope that won't be a problem..."

I smiled at her and lit up a cigarette. "*Beautiful dreamer, queen of my song,*" I half-sang to her. She smiled faintly. I added, "An old song my mother used to sing sitting at the piano, when I was a boy."

"Yeah, Stephen Foster, I knew it, too," Boots chimed in. It was contagious, for then he started singing. "*Gone from the earth to a better land I know. I hear the gentle voices callin', Ol' Black Joe....* Them songs were from the heart. What happened to 'em?" Even in his terrible gruff voice, the old song of the South sounded sentimental, as if the tune had in it the right ingredients, so that whoever was singing it would give it meaning.

Then it was Eleanor's turn. "My favorite is, '*Oh the sun shines bright on my ol' Kentucky home, my ol' Kentucky home far away...Weep no more, my ladies.... Weep no more today, I will sing my song for my ol' Kentucky home, my ol' Kentucky home far away....*" Then Eleanor began to cry. "Zorrie and I used sing that song!"

I went over to her. "Hey…kid, I miss her too and I hardly knew her. You know, you still gotta pretty voice like that afternoon at the Firefly, remember? Boots and I sound like sick cats compared to you." I held her and let her head fall onto my lapel. Sometimes tears just have to come and there's no way to hold 'em back. They're like a treasury of things saved up, everything— the experiences we stuff in the back drawer until it's payday. Then we have to face that music and let the tears come. Maybe not today, or even tomorrow, but one day I knew that I, too, would have to unleash all that cache stuffed into my head and guts.

"I gotta ditch my car if I'm staying here with you." I took Eleanor's arm and led her into the bedroom. I sat her down quietly and gently kissed the tears that had fallen and settled upon her lips. "Be right back, babe."

I started for my car around the block, but I never made it. A sap hit me on the back of the head and I went down for the count, careening down into that black, spinning world of the unconscious. Next thing I knew I was in a smelly, dark room, the kind of place you figure you *don't* go if you've squared it with St. Peter. I could see a slit of light somewhere through a partly open door at the top of some stairs. My head was still swimming. Someone had tied me to some water pipes, so I figured I was in a basement somewhere.

Just then the door opened and a familiar voice shouted down at me. "You're a bad penny, Denning. You keep showing up in the wrong places at the wrong times. Did you think I didn't know you were shacking up with Eleanor at your old ex-cop buddy's place? And we have plans for them, too."

"I'll bust your face open if you harm either of those two, Berguson."

"My, my, how hostile. Give me the *electra*-strip and you're home free. All of you. Until tonight. It's Tuesday and you've been out since Sunday, in case you were wondering. I have a habit of repeatedly hitting a man when he's down, Denning. It's in, shall we say, my nature. Think it over. I'll be back in an hour. Then...time's up for all of us, even private dicks."

He slammed the door, leaving me mostly in the dark again. The ropes that bound me to the pipes were thick, but sinewy. I swiped my feet back and forth on the gravel floor. Nothing. Then I tried to stand by sliding my hands up the pipe as I went. This time I was in luck. Although I couldn't see it, I could feel a safety spigot about three feet up. I began rubbing the rope against the sharper edges of the handle. Lucky for me, the rope was a bit frayed. I worked slowly but desperately to free myself. Finally the strands became unraveled and I sawed myself free.

Now I had to take care of Berguson. I realized I had never seen his face—I only heard his voice. But wait, I thought. Tomorrow's Wednesday. Meeting day at Forest Lawn! I had to sneak out the basement window and hit the road, and be there when Berguson met with Mr. Mysterious tomorrow. I found the window, unlatched it and slowly pried it open. It barely opened enough to slide my body through, but I just managed to squeeze out. I scrambled up some terrain to level ground and ran as fast as I could to a main street. I found a liquor store and rushed in to use the phone. The clerk gestured to the back where the payphone hung on the wall like a welcomed lifeline.

Nervously I dialed Boots' number. The old fart answered. "Yeah? This better be who I think it better be."

"Boots! It's Cable...get yourself and Eleanor out of the house immediately. Berguson sapped me and told me he knows about you and that Eleanor is there. Tell Eleanor I'm shaken up a bit with sore wrists, but I'm okay."

"She's goin' crazy with worry for ya, Cable. Here, talk to her."

"Darling, darling!" Eleanor cried. "You're alive! I thought—

"—Not yet, angel. Berguson clunked me a good one last night on my way to the car...but I think somebody up there likes me and—"

"—Somebody down here likes you, too. Oh, Cable...what shall we do? This can't go on! They'll kill you, I know they will! I don't know how much longer I can take this insane not knowing!"

"Tell Boots to go to Code House Three, babe, he'll know what I mean. Wait there until I catch up with you tomorrow evening, if all goes well. I've got a date with Berguson at that Forest Lawn David statue at 4:00 p.m. You got that, angel?"

"Yes, oh, yes! I beg you, Cable, come back to me!"

I hung up remembering I hadn't eaten a thing in two days. But cheapskate that I am, I decided to catch a cab, pick up my little Dodge coupe and head back to my office, where I hadn't been in a couple days. When I got to my car, the first thing I checked was under the rug on the driver's side. Yep, the *electra*-strip was still there.

Only an idiot would stash something so valuable there. But I felt they figured me smarter than that. So I had hoped they'd never look for it in such an obvious place.

The refrigerator had some old chili I knew I had to eat soon. I checked things out carefully before I stepped into my inner sanctum. There was a package, addressed to me, lying at the top of the landing in front of my door. I lifted it and the damn thing was as heavy as hell. I took it inside and placed it on my desk. Then I dug into that chili con carne like a miner who had been six months out of food. I wandered over to the package. There was no return address. I opened it. There staring at me in the face was Madam Zorrie Robles' crystal ball! There was also a note: *"Cable, Mediums have ways of knowing. I would have survived my injuries, but I'm afraid there's more to come. I'm sending you my precious crystal orb. Please take good care of it. If what I sense comes true, by the time you get this package I may no longer be on the earthly dimension. I don't know why they want to kill me. I don't have what they want. Maybe it's karmic. I'll try to get out of town as soon as I can, but if I don't make it, use the crystal ball to get hold of me from the other side. I can still guide you, fondly, Zorrie Robles."*

If I'd had false teeth they would've fallen out. Poor Zorrie. She was one of the oddest, yet charming, gals I'd ever had the pleasure to know, albeit briefly. This grand dame of the occult died for something I started. Yet I knew so little about the whole damn mess myself. Well, maybe you could say Fredericka Winston started it—I just said yes. My pain and frustration hit like a huge rubber mallet in the gut...the kind of feeling ya get when guilt and disbelief hit you at the same time, and when things you helped to start get outta control and you wish they hadn't!

I took the crystal ball and wrapped it carefully in a blanket. I'd have to hide it somewhere where it was safe. The *electra*-strip was okay in the coupe for now. Where to put Zorrie's crystal ball? There was a loose panel behind my bedstead. I carefully removed it, tucked the crystal orb between the two-by-fours and did a quick repair job on the panel so it'd look undisturbed. I fell onto my bed. I knew I could easily just fall asleep...but better not. Berguson was missing me about now and I knew he'd be determined to turn over every leaf and every stone looking for me. And if he found me, he would employ his best methods to find out where that strip was and *then* kill me. It was late. I had a part-time secretary, Ida Latney, a pretty young thing I hired for a buck an hour when I could afford her. She'd take me in. I went to my desk and dug up her phone number. It rang at the other end like a solitary pulse through a lonely night, the kind that wraps around the inside of your head and reminds you how out of touch with life and other people you can get when you're in the bad-guy-chasing business.

"Hello..." a very sleepy female voice said at the other end.

"Hello, Ida?"

"Yes...."

"This is Cable Denning, your some-times employer. I'm in a pinch and I have some pretty mean characters chasin' me. I need a place to stay for the night...I'm sorry to call you so late...but I didn't know who else to call. I can't stay at my office tonight."

"Mr. Denning! Are you hurt?"

"Well, that's debatable, Ida. I've been slugged, zapped and roughed up for a couple of days, but I think I've got all my teeth and most of my brains. At least I can talk," I said, making an attempt to make light of the situation.

"Yes, you may stay on my sofa. I have a roommate and she'll have to know. But I won't tell anyone else."

"Say, that's swell of you, Ida. I won't forget it. By the way, I have some work for you. Are you available next week?"

"Yes. I was hoping you'd call one day soon. I could sure use the work with the war and all."

"Give me your address. I've got a feeling I gotta get out of this place pronto."

"I'm at the Alto Nido Apts. 1851 Ivar, #206. It's just down from your office above Yucca. I'll be up."

I thanked her and left my office post haste. I knew Ida Latney had a soft spot for me. Guys can pick up that sort of thing. Sometimes I'd catch her looking at me when I was on the phone. When dames get a look like that, it's every man for himself out the exit. But I liked Ida....she wasn't a pushy kind of dame and had never given me a reason to think she was anything but a straight arrow. I threw a few pieces of clean laundry in a pillowcase and remembered that my 'necessaries' were still in the coupe from my Santa Barbara trip with Eleanor.

By the time I arrived at Ida's she had awakened herself somewhat with a cup of coffee. She offered me some, but I declined knowing that sleep was what I needed.

"Welcome, Mr. Denning, to my humble little place." She was a petite blonde with blue eyes and a cute snub nose. Her skin was mid-western white and she had the look of a fresh young girl who was still seventeen, tho' I knew she had turned twenty-seven last year. We had celebrated her birthday at Johnny's Steakhouse on Hollywood Blvd.. She had a great little figure, too, you knew inside her bra were tight, well-packed medium-sized breasts, topped off with good skin, great teeth and a hell of a smile.

"Well, thanks, Ida. It's been a hell of a week for me. I'm just glad you were home and that you answered the phone."

Ida chided me. "At 1:30 in the morning? Where would I go, Mr. Denning?"

"Well...well...I thought you might have a nice young man and decided to stay over or something. Well, you know."

"I'm not that kind of girl, Mr. Denning. You know that." She scolded me slightly.

"Yeah, I guess I do, don't I," I answered somewhat sheepishly.

We exchanged a few words. "Ida, I hope I'm not taking advantage of you or anything."

"Oh, no, Mr. Denning." She looked me over carefully, catching a glimpse of a pretty beat up guy whacking his way through this nutso world. "Are you hungry or anything?"

I looked at the lovely little creature. "Nah, but thanks just the same, Ida. But to tell you the truth," I said yawning. "I gotta grab some shut eye here."

"Oh, of course, Mr. Denning. I laid out a pillow and some blankets. I hope you'll be comfortable on my sofa."

"Uh, yeah I'll be fine and thanks again, Ida."

"You can stay here as long as you need to." Her voice showed concern.

"Thanks, Ida, but I've got a date with Michelangelo's *David* tomorrow afternoon. I mean the statue, of course.

"That's strange. Isn't that in a cemetery or something?"

"Yeah, Forest Lawn, that place where the ritzy go when the roll is called up yonder.

"Well, good night then."

"Good night, Ida." She disappeared down the hall and I collapsed on her old, worn-out couch. I was out like a light. The last thought I had was of me searching amongst tombstones for a large statue of Michelangelo's *David*. Tomorrow would be a hell of a day. I just knew it. And I'd get to see who Berguson was playing footsie with—the terrible Mr. X.

Chapter 6

ONEX FOUR AND THE KLIX-STRIP

I stopped at the information gate to Forest Lawn at 1712 South Glendale Blvd., about 3:30 p.m. on that fateful Wednesday. It was one of those days in L.A. when the smell of automobile exhaust hung like old pans of burnt oil in the air and from the hills of Glendale one could hardly see downtown.

The rather snooty custodian looked at my beat-up Dodge coupe and the guy inside with the unshaven face and winced internally. He was that type of person that didn't ever want you to touch him for fear some dust of the common folk would rub off on him. He told me this was a prestigious joint since 1917 and was patrolled by someone who probably looked like Boots Blake and could move just about as fast. He told me I could find the statue of Michelangelo's *David* over on the west side about three-quarters of the way up the hill. Forest Lawn was like a memorial city, roads and side roads all over the place. Some were even paved. Famous movie stars, politicians, the rich and famous as well as the unknown were buried here. As long as you could afford it, you were in.

As I drove towards my destination, I remembered again that I had actually never seen Berguson's face. I knew his body type. But he was either attacking me from behind, hiding behind a wall with a revolver or standing silhouetted upstairs from me in that basement he tossed me into. I had plenty of grudge against this

109

guy. I wouldn't need much of an excuse to take him down either.

David stood on a stone patio backed by a few trees. Marble benches waited in the shade for anyone who cared to take a load off of their feet or sit and meditate for a while. Yeah, I needed to do that. I was still a bit numb from Zorrie's unnecessary murder and I was carrying some anger and revenge to Forest Lawn that day. I knew I had to approach the statue from behind. But that wouldn't be easy. Some grottos like David's were isolated and fenced in the back to keep people from tramping all over the movie stars' graves while they did the Hollywood tourist thing. Above all, I'd be dead if I was spotted. Berguson and Mr. X would see to that.

I found a hidden clump of bushes and trees just south of the grotto. Precisely at 4:03 p.m., a weasel-like little man strolled toward the statue as if he were a sightseer. He had short-cropped black hair and wore a fine pinstripe suit. He had a pinched nose and quick, darting eyes. Another young couple had meandered into the grotto to study the sixteen-foot statue that to my uncultured eyes looked just like the *David* I'd seen in art books. The presence of the young people perturbed our Mr. X and he kept looking up at the statue and then at them until finally they wandered off. Just then I got my first straight-on look at the burly Leon Berguson. Not a bad looking chap, I thought, someone Fredericka could definitely have bedded. But he was angry and walked fast toward Mr. X. They sat at the bench closest to the statue and quietly argued. Mr. X was most decidedly not pleased at Berguson's recent failures to bump me off and rescue the *electra*-strip.

Then a strange thing happened. Mr. X pointed a gun at Berguson from his coat pocket and urged him toward a big black Lincoln sitting at the curb just outside the grotto. Mr. X coaxed Berguson into the back seat of the automobile. I knew I had to move now. I heard a couple of shots. As quick as I could negotiate, I went lunging toward the Lincoln. As I got to the driver's side, I ripped open the door and drew out my .38 and waved it wildly at both men before they could fire at me. "All right, Berguson and Mr. whoever you are...throw down your heat and put your hands behind your head!" I blurted with authority. But Berguson seemed knocked out.

Mr. X did exactly as I ordered him and threw down a Luger with a large silencer. "No concern, Mr. Denning. Besides now, there is only *one* of us to worry about." I glanced back at Berguson. A nice clean bullet hole in the middle of his forehead told me little Mr. X meant business. "Mr. Berguson and I had a difference of opinion. You see, now he's...he's, well, what shall I say...resting on the premises of Forest Lawn. Appropriate, don't you think, Mr. Denning?"

"Look, buddy, I don't know who you are or where you came from...but I want out of this mess! I'm a private dick with no intention of putting my life on the line for—"

"—then why don't you simply give me the *Klix*-strip?"

I sidled onto the front seat, my gun trained at Mr. X's head. I thought for a second. "What the hell is that and what makes you think I've got it Mr...Mr—?"

"—Krieger...Anton Krieger, Mr. Denning." He smiled an evil smile at me. "Come, come now. We mustn't play games, you and I. You found the item quite by accident that afternoon at Miss Winston's abode. As usual, Berguson was late and inept. Besides, he's worn out his usefulness to us."

So...finally I found out who "K" was on the note in Berguson's trashcan. In a way I was glad to see Berguson dead as a doornail in the backseat. I owed him a few, but maybe not the whole shebang! "Us? Who's us?" I asked, knowing somehow I was getting deeper and deeper into the sludge that was crawling up my pant leg like a disease I couldn't stop.

"All in good time, Mr. Denning. I suggest, since you have me at a great disadvantage...and I certainly did not expect you today...that you move over and let me take you to Miss Winston and Dr. Carlton Zelbacher."

That was the best but riskiest offer I'd had all day. After I confiscated his gun and shoved Berguson's body down flat on the back seat of the car, I moved to the passenger side and Krieger drove off. We went west for at least an hour, ending up somewhere north of Malibu.

"I adore the ocean, don't you, Mr. Denning?" Krieger was saying with just enough German accent to make his voice smooth and syrupy. "I was raised near the Baltic Sea. Most pleasant memories of childhood."

"Hard to imagine you were ever a child, Krieger. Guys like you are a type I've met up with before. They go around making up for what they don't have by taking what belongs to someone else. And they don't mind bumping off whoever's in the way."

"How very perceptive you are. You forgot one thing, however."

"What's that?"

"A certain kind of genius mixed with an unwell personality. One, shall we say, who was arrested at quite a young age. So, one might say, Mr. Denning, I am a brilliant misfit."

"So I guess that's where someone like me comes in. As nuts as it sounds, every once in a while I stop taking photos of philandering husbands and wives and go after guys like you that have stepped into the really dark shadows. You know why? Because you're the ones that generate the plague of lust, power and money in the world, control populations like pawns on a chessboard and start wars for profit."

"Provocative, Mr. Denning. I think I might even like you under different circumstances. Your peasant mind has at least a modicum of ability to decipher truth from fiction about the world. But you see, it is all in vain. The rich and powerful own you. From birth. They will always own you and set you into motion like little wind-up toys to do their bidding."

"There's gotta be right from wrong, Krieger. And someone's gotta care or else all there'll be is chaos."

"But chaos is what we *intend*, my dear private investigator. You see, Mr. Denning, you are like most of the human race. You pretend your shit doesn't stink and every time you take a crap you're ashamed, afraid to admit you're an animal so you pretend. Until the next time when you have to repeat the humiliating process." Krieger's voice was rabid but controlled. "Women, who consume most of the toilet paper in the world, are very good at it. They conceal their smelly orifices with perfume and mannerism. Child birth is such a painful surprise for them, for it is here they come face to face with the all-animal self."

"Maybe only part animal, Krieger," I said, defying this man whose own bitterness had carved him into a frozen, malicious thing. "Don't you ever have an inkling that there's something better? I don't mean religious. I mean like *cosmic*...like what about all those sloughed off aircraft or spacecraft sightings lately? The one here and the really strange one in Cape Girardeau...don't you ever wonder, Krieger? What if there are beings who don't piss and shit, don't war on each other, don't screw each other for money?"

Krieger looked at me as he pulled off Highway One onto a side road. "Mr. Denning! I am amazed! How could a little peon brain like yours think such things? Now I see, it is no accident that you have become embroiled in our quest."

"Quest?"

"You'll see soon enough. Patience, Mr. Denning."

I smiled to myself as I lit a cigarette. It wore me out, but I enjoyed lighting into him. Krieger was the sort of guy you found in movie roles, the arch villain who finally had no conscience. Because that isn't what he was about. "Since we're doin' true confessions, Krieger, can you answer me a couple of questions about how I got into this mess in the first place?"

"If I can," he said in that gentile voice that bespoke of a European cultured background.

"What was in the envelope Berguson hit me over the head for?"

"Money, what else? Berguson was a tough-boy dandy. He romanced Fredericka Winston to get to Dr. Zelbacher. Then he purposely disappeared when their love affair was at its peak, so naturally Miss Winston hired someone to find him."

"That would be me."

"Precisely. Then she talked her sister Eleanor into lending her enough money to pay you, but Mrs. Zelbacher was reluctant."

"So she promised me the moon but paid me peanuts. But what I don't figure, is once I found Berguson, where did Fredericka get the dough for that escapade...and why meet at some remote, deserted place on Lanterman Terrace?"

"By then our dear corpse in the back seat had found out from Fredericka that Carlton, Dr. Zelbacher, had one of the *Klix*-strips. So he began to blackmail the Winston sisters by promising he would not tell anyone what Dr. Zelbacher was doing in his hidden laboratory. And of course he did not wish to be seen, hence the different location."

"Why all this, when he worked for you in the first place?"

"You see, Mr. Denning, greed is a terrible thing when it becomes short-sighted. We paid Berguson well. But he wanted more on the side for himself. And you know the rest."

"Who hid the strip and why?"

"Let's just say that when Dr. Zelbacher returned to work in *our* laboratory, *involuntarily* I might add, we were minus one *Klix*-strip. Did he hide it? Or did one of the sisters? Or someone else?"

"So why kidnap both Carlton and Fredericka? Did they know too much already?"

"Too many questions, Mr. Denning. I'm afraid you shall discover all those answers *after the fact*, shall we say?"

"All right, swell. Just one more question. How many more layers do we have to go through until we meet the real brains behind this whole scientific abracadabra?"

"None. I'm as high as it goes...on the human plane."

I shut up. Krieger's last words were calculated to hit me like a ten-pound hammer in the chest. And they did. My gut thing was acting up again and I was beginning to piece together all the recent 'extra-terrestrial sightings and alien spacecraft.' "Remember, Krieger, I've still got the gun...and you don't. So keep your behavior on the up and up. Don't think I'd have any compunction against bumping you off, if it came to it."

"As you wish, Mr. Denning," he said quietly.

We drove another twenty minutes. It was dusk by the time we wound down a steep road and came head-on to a gate. An old wooden sign read, *Trancas House* above one of the two pillars between which the locked gate stood. A tall fellow with a thin black mustache came to the window as Krieger opened it. "Wie gehts, Fritz. Herr Denning ist mit mir...und Berguson...er ist in der rückseite.....tot."

"What'd you say? I don't speak kraut."

"I told him you were with me and Berguson is in the back, dead."

We drove ahead toward a medium-sized house set among some hedges and Eucalyptus trees. Once we parked, someone else took the car with Leon Berguson's body in it and we walked into a rather cozy middle-class American home. But how wrong can one be? Krieger went directly to what looked like a closet door. I followed Krieger in, looking for a double-cross at any turn. That closet we stepped into was a damn elevator! Krieger pressed a button and down we went. The door opened to a flurry of activity with men and women in white coats everywhere. Krieger led me to a large door at the end of a hallway.

"You realize, Mr. Denning, what you are now witnessing makes it impossible for you to ever leave here alive."

"Let me be the judge of that, Krieger," I said, thrusting the barrel of my .38 into his side through my coat pocket. "Uh, quite a set up you've got here."

We entered the large door and were greeted by two huge men who looked like German wrestlers. Krieger motioned them to go. But I saw them close the door behind and then remain just outside the door waiting, no doubt, for a signal from their boss to pounce on me if and when the opportunity arose.

Krieger took off his coat and tie and slumped into a huge chair behind a desk. "You exasperate me, Mr. Denning. You just might be smarter and braver than I gave you credit for."

"Well, that sounds like it could be a compliment, Mr. Krieger," I said with a little salt in my voice as I lit up a cigarette. "You just might be smarter than I thought, too."

"Well, isn't that nice? That makes two of us. Would you like a drink before I show you what you came here for?"

117

"I dunno. How can I be sure it ain't made up of some fatal ingredients concocted right here in your Nazi laboratories?"

"That's not, uh.....what do you say...my *style*, Mr. Denning. Do not insult me. Let me assure you. I always enjoy showing new things to anyone who has as much interest as you do in things that go...uh...*bump in the night*."

Somehow I believed the guy and I threw down two stiff drinks of some of the best Scotch whiskey I'd sampled in years. "Not bad liquor, Krieger."

"Have as much as you like. The bar is open to you."

"No thanks. Two is my limit when I'm...I'm on duty, to quote another American saying."

Krieger frowned. "As you wish."

Just then a comely young woman escorted a small boy into the office. He was obviously East Indian with very dark skin and those big black/brown eyes that have probably been used often to captivate the hearts of many young Indian women whenever the notion struck. After he greeted Krieger, he approached me. "Hello, Mr. Denning. I am Lareet Pajabbi. I know of you from Miss Fredericka."

"Pleased to meet you, Lareet. Quite a fancy place ya got goin' here," I laughed, trying to think up something.

"Yes. This is the land of experiments."

"You don't say. By the way, how *is* Miss Fredericka?"

" Oh, she is well. She will join us later. But right now she is on her sleep pill..."

Krieger threw Lareet a dirty look as if the kid wasn't supposed to say that. But it passed quickly. "Good." I said. "I will be pleased to see her. It's been quite some time."

"Uncle Anton wants me to show you something. So, if you'll come with me, I would be very pleased," Lareet informed me.

Uncle Anton? Krieger wanted to stay behind, but since he was sort of attached to the end of my gun, I urged him to join us.

We walked through a long hallway. But as we got further and further along, it got hotter and very humid. Pretty soon I was sweating enough to start my own greenhouse. I took my coat off but kept my hand in the right pocket. Krieger was not impressed. Then we came to a room that had a very eerie green glow to it, as if the light was fluorescent but had no obvious source.

Soon we entered another, inner chamber. There leaning against a small metal table stood something right off a page from Campbell's Astounding Science Fiction! "Mr. Denning, I would like you to meet Onex Four." This strange little creature had a head, two arms that terminated in three fingers each, two legs. But other than that he was alien from head to toe. His eyes were long slits out of which sparkled pitch-black eyes. He had what seemed like a mouth...small, thin with no perceptible lips. The nasal passages lay flat against his face and his skin was a greenish-white. He wore no clothes and no sexual organs were visible.

I didn't know what to do. I looked to Lareet for tips. "Can I approach him?"

"Oh. It is well. But do not touch him. We have many germs on our skin. He may become ill."

I urged Krieger out in front of me as we approached *Onex Four*. "Good to meet you, *Onex Four*," I said, scrambling for words. "Are you able to speak our language? "

Krieger walked a few feet forward and turned a dial and something like a radio set started crackling in the room. "No. But he is so clever he has allowed us to build a translator from his thoughts...to our words."

"Welcome...Mr. Denning...why are you so afraid? You possess a killing weapon in your clothing. Why is this so?"

The damn creature had x-ray vision as well! "Well, it's this way, kid...you see, fear is a part of the human experience, and not all humans are who they say they are...and...well they mean to do harm to others."

"Yet who harms you here? I welcome you. I do not have harmful intentions, Mr. Denning. I am told you have the second Klix-silicon strip. Is this so?"

The kid was sharp. "How old are you, Onex? Are you able to trust your fellow beings?"

"I am four-hundred of your years, but I am about the same age as Lareet here on your planet. I must return to the subject of the Klix-silicon strip. We seek it because it is the only way I can be teleported back to the circling hovercraft of my fellow beings, as you call them. We are multi-dimensional creatures. When we crashed on your planet, my three companions perished and much of our technical equipment was destroyed. Dr. Zelbacher has one Klix-silicon strip he is repairing for us. When he is finished he will need the second Klix-strip to accelerate the silicon-trios generation speed. Can you hear me, Mr. Denning? "

"I don't get it, Onex. Don't you see? They're misleading you. Do you think they're gonna let you go home?

120

Earth people are greedy, dishonest, self-serving and if they can gain power or make a buck, or capitalize on your technology, they're gonna do it, regardless of some nice young...young..."

"Klix. We are called the Klix, Mr. Denning. What you say to me rings true to my mind. We have long studied earth beings, especially your species. And they are oddly misleading."

Krieger bounded to the translator and shut it down. "I think you are over-taxing the boy, Mr. Denning. He needs rest now. We'll speak with him later." Krieger excused Lareet and the attendants. I shook the little Indian's hand, thanked him for being a good guide, returned his smile and we started back towards Krieger's office.

"So where did you get space boy?" I asked to get a rise out of Krieger.

"He...he, ah, came to us...by way of a spacecraft crash last spring in Missouri."

"Oh. That's strange. Don't remember hearing about it." Then it hit me. He said his *3 companions perished!* Only three bodies were reported at Cape Girardeau...the krauts must have stolen Onex Four from the site. In surviving the crash, the little alien became prisoner and the ideal specimen of study for Hitler's underground madmen. "Seems like unidentified flying objects are dashing to earth like falling stars. I wonder what else we don't know."

"You'd be surprised, Mr. Denning."

"So ya finally did it. Found one alive so you can exploit the hell out of him and then throw him away when you're through, is that it, Krieger?"

"Mr. Denning! You disturb my finer sensibilities when you say such things. Just because you don't consider me as having much 'humanity,' or whatever you call it, I am very personally interested in other beings from other solar systems, and perhaps other dimensions ... a possible improvement over humans."

"I see. Well, that puts it right now, doesn't it?"

"Despite your negative thoughts toward me, I still have to live with myself, you know."

"I didn't know you had a real self to live with, Krieger. I thought guys like you connive without conscience until you get what you want. I saw how nonchalantly you plugged Berguson. Bang! It's over...and you're on to the next project. What's it feel like to be a member of the project-of-the-month club? How many people die along the way...and just how much money and power do you stow away for a rainy day to take care of that 'real self' you live with?"

"Why so testy, Mr. Denning? We all teeter between rationality and insanity. Do you think you are an exception?"

"No, but I'm not dimented enough to blow people away just because they're in your way or not useful anymore...like that poor sap Berguson. I told you before, Krieger, I know your type of man. They grow 'em on trees in broad daylight. Alcatraz is full of 'em."

We got to Krieger's office door. "I'm sorry you feel such rancor for me, Mr. Private Detective. Pity. I was actually growing fond of your frank and acid ways." His tone was sardonic.

"Take me to Fredericka and ol' Doc Zelbacher."

"Now?"

"Yes, now." I knew that time was running out and that I only had so much of it to do what I came for.

"I hope you're not pushing me…"

"I *am* pushing you, Krieger. Seeing is believing. Lead on."

Reluctantly Krieger led us through another maze of hallways and turns. Finally he knocked at a door. A frazzled and dazed Fredericka opened it. I knew the dame had been doped, but she seemed to recognize me. "Mr. Denning! Mr. Denning…." Then she glanced at Krieger. "I…I, uh…I'm a mess. I am glad to see you. Won't you come in?"

" Well, hello, Miss Winston. I was hoping you might throw something on and come have a drink with Doctor Zelbacher and us."

She had a puzzled look in her face. "Who?"

"The doc. You remember…Eleanor's long lost hubby?" I said sarcastically.

"Oh, you mean Carlton. Yes, I'll be with you in a moment. Is that all right with you, Mr. Krieger?"

Krieger looked at me and frowned as he glanced at the gun in my pocket pointing at him. "Uh…yes, Fredericka. That would be nice. A nice toast to welcome Mr. Denning…would be appropriate."

Minutes later we entered a darkened laboratory. A small East Indian woman approached us. "Yes, what can I do, Mr. Krieger…?"

"We want to see Dr. Zelbacher. Is he in?"

The woman looked at Fredericka and me strangely. "Yes, but I don't think he's able…"

I nudged my gun into Krieger's back. "Take us to him," Krieger ordered. "By the way, Mr. Denning, this is Sereba, Lareet's mother."

"Pleased to meet you. You have quite a son. I enjoy bright young people."

Mrs. Pajabbi thanked me. But she was sad, dull, and displayed a hopelessness, probably from a long time ago. As we walked toward the end of the laboratory, I was wondering how I'd feel facing Carlton Zelbacher. I wasn't in the habit of bedding other men's wives. Especially when the nature of my business taught me how tawdry and second-class it could be. I knew that men and women escape the confines of marriage to find something that was always missing from the relationship, or to round it out, or in search of that other half that would make them whole. Sereba Pajabbi knocked on a large red door. "Doctor, Doctor, " she called.

"Go away, Sereba! I don't want you to see me! Please....just go away."

Her voice was gentle, as if she had a special attachment to the man behind the door. "But Doctor, there are some important people here to see you."

"There *are* no more important people. Buzz them off, Sereba. Then please come rub my back."

It sounded like the doc had been drinking or he, too, was drugged up like Fredericka. I urged the gun deeper into Krieger's ribs. "Doctor Zelbacher, it is I, Anton Krieger. I have a special guest here."

"You least of all, Krieger. I hate you. I hate what you're doing here. I hate the cruel senselessness of you Nazis. I even hate the disparity of light-years separating us from... from them."

Krieger looked at me and shrugged. "I don't think he likes me today, Mr. Denning...." At least I knew Eleanor's husband was not a Nazi sympathizer.

Just then Fredericka started pounding on the door. "Carlton, it's me...Fred...come on, let me in. I know you'll like this man. Besides, he has a message from Eleanor."

There was a silence. "Eleanor?" There was a rustling behind the door and soon a tall, gaunt man opened the door. His hair was bright silver, his eyes an intense golden-brown. He looked old for his years. I figured him to be no more than fifty, but he looked seventy, if a day. He looked at everyone with a rather blank stare. "Who knows about Eleanor? I don't even know about Eleanor anymore now, do I?"

"I'm Cable Denning, Dr. Zelbacher. I'm a private investigator. Fredericka and your wife hired me a few days back to help them find you. Now we found you. Do you want to come home now?"

Carlton Zelbacher looked at Krieger who was obviously not happy with the question I put to the doctor. "I can't....I cannot...I can't go home now...I'm...I'm no longer...what...what I used to be."

I felt pity for this man who was under great stress and most likely drugged by Krieger to keep him subdued enough to do his bidding. "What're you afraid of, doc? I'm sure if you decide to come with Fredericka and me now, today, Mr. Krieger will have no objection. Tomorrow may be too late."

With his mouth hung open, he swayed before us, trying to focus in on me. "I cannot, Mr. Denning. Thanks for helping the girls—they're good girls, you know."

A pain of guilt ran through me. "Yeah, I know, doc, they're both swell girls."

Zelbacher looked knowingly over at Krieger. "I have to stay...because my work is almost done. I want Onex Four to go home. Did someone bring the other *Klix*-strip?"

Seemed like everyone down here knew that I might have brought the *Klix*-strip or whatever it was. "Would it save your life if I did bring it? Far as I can figure, doc, you and all the rest of the swabs on this deck are scared to death of this guy," I said, pointing my gun at Krieger. "But you know what? He's just as mortal as you and I. He can die just as easily."

"It's not Krieger, Mr. Denning. It's the work. I'm far too involved. Too much to explain. Just get me the strip. Now, please.....go! Take Fred with you and go! It's too late for me." Then he slammed the door in front of us. Sereba Pajabbi began to cry. I could tell by those tears she was in love with him. She was probably his only link to sanity. I noticed Fredericka's eyes were not all that dry either.

"So you see, Mr. Denning," Krieger said, fluffing himself up a bit. "The doctor is not being coerced to perform...his scientific tasks. In fact, he rather likes what he does...and what he's becoming...."

That had an ominous note to it. "Becoming what, Krieger?" I took my gun out and pinned him against the wall. Fredericka cried out, "Mr. Denning, think of Carlton, please." I stuck the barrel of the .38 deep in his fat gut. "Don't look now, but your slime is running out of you, spreading all over the place like a fatal disease to anyone who buys into your bullshit!"

Krieger was trembling a bit, but he still held on to his determination. "I...I hope...I sincerely hope, Mr. Denning, I shall have the opportunity to dispose of you one day. So, politely, and in the best possible sense, I warn you...you are all dead...all of you...your Eleanor, that terrible old man with the growl in his voice who calls you friend, Fredericka...and maybe even that comely little secretary in your office this morning who's tidying up for you."

How could he know about Ida Latney? She must have figured I needed help cleaning up my joint...and *they* must have spies everywhere. I crossed my mental fingers that they had not followed Boots and Eleanor to the secret hideout. But I would call Krieger's bluff anyway. "*What* is the doc becoming? If you don't answer I'll blow off your knees, then your crotch." Fredericka squeaked and Mrs. Pajabbi put her hand across her mouth in fear.

That seemed to do the trick. Krieger's eyes grew wide, the whites showing like an unsuspecting calf just before the slaughter. "One of *them*. He's injecting himself with alien genetic code serum. He wants to go with Onex Four. But he will not succeed."

It had been a long, hard day. Since I left Ida's apartment it had been a roller coaster of events not likely to fit on a page of a "dear diary." From the strange meeting at Forest Lawn, to Berguson's cold-blooded murder by Krieger, to the strange closet-elevator that took us down to a science fiction wonderland, including the meeting of my first *Klix*....and the whole strange lot down here in this scientific denizen.

I backed up my gun a little and the women relaxed. So did Krieger as he recomposed himself. "I'll tell you what, Krieger, I'll make a little deal with you. You escort Fredericka and me back to my car at Forest Lawn. You give me twenty-four hours to think over what I should do with that damn *Klix*-strip."

"You may not last that long, Mr. Denning. My people are out there. Everywhere. They will find you. They will find the strip. You can't win. None of you can. We are always superior."

"Well...why not let's test that theory, Krieger. Start walking toward that elevator, tough guy. Let's see what that German fiber inside you is really made of. Show me you and your Hitler Youth don't have flaws...don't have holes in your perfect Arian nation. Are you with me, Miss Winston?"

"Right behind you, Mr. Denning."

"You will be taken down, Mr. Denning, sooner or later."

"Maybe, pal, but not tonight. As I said, drop us back at my car, give me twenty-four hours to think things over. In case I decide to come back with the strip, you give me a through-line to your telephone."

"And if I make this so-called *deal* and you decide *not* to come back with the strip...can you see the position that puts me in?"

"That's somethin' *you* gotta bite off and chew, Krieger. I've got my own problems and right now you're one of 'em."

I said good-bye to Sereba Pajabbi and we started for the elevator. I noticed three of Krieger's giant goons following us. Fredericka was shaking.

"Will we get out alive?

"I don't know. Hang on tight." I had a hunch the dope they'd given her was wearing off. We reached the elevator and the goons stopped coming. We rode up in silence. When the door opened, Krieger looked at me with those beady little eyes of his. "Only because you've had a loaded gun pointed at me for the past few hours do I go along with this...and of course there is the hope of possession...err....obtainment of the *Klix*-strip. So, you have your twenty-four hours. If the strip is not in my possession by then, Mr. Denning, consider yourself, Fredericka and Eleanor Winston and your old man friend *dead*. And how do I know you will not turn the strip over the American government...now that you are aware of its significance?"

"Ha! Do you think I can trust them any more than you? This government is filled with infiltration, perversions, spies and anti-spies, secretive and corrupt power and moneygrubbers at every level. I don't care what branch you choose...from the White House to the Supreme Court. Crooks and criminals are everywhere, Krieger, in every country."

"My, my—hit a nerve, did I?" Krieger sniggered at me. "Well, that bit puts my mind at ease, at least." He studied me. "And despite your being an American elitist, somehow I don't think you're one to....as you say...sell-out."

We traveled an hour and a half back to Forest Lawn. It was almost dawn. The damn gate was closed. It was a wooden affair with a light bolt-lock. "Jam the engine, Krieger, we're goin' through.

129

He floor-boarded that powerful Lincoln and we flattened the gate in seconds. "You'll pay for the damages to this car as well, Mr. Denning. I hate flagrant vandalism."

"You might keep that in mind before you decide to kill me off."

Fredericka interrupted, "Please don't goad him, Mr. Denning. He's a killer."

"Well, I'll simply have to find a way to collect first." Krieger said smugly."

We got to my coupe, still parked where I left it. But there was a green violation ticket on it. "Now, Krieger, I want you to wait for Fredericka and me to get in and we're gonna follow you out of this place, understand? Then I'm going to make sure you go back the way you came for as many miles as I need to. If you so much as turn off the road to pee, I'll blast your windows out and hope I hit you in the process. Is that clear or do I need to send you a telegram?"

"Clear, Mr. Denning. I'll be seeing you...as the song goes."

As Fredericka and I got out, Krieger sent me a look. Well, you know the saying...if looks could kill....

We got in, I started up my little Dodge and we followed the Lincoln. I tailed him for about fifteen minutes until I knew we had bought enough time to hightail it for Code House Three. That was all we had now. We had no more secret places left to hide out in, without them getting wind of it. I wasn't even sure they didn't know about this one. I still didn't know who 'they' were—more than likely foreign government agencies or wealthy concerns, bent on making a pretty mint from the technology hidden in the hills above Trancas Beach.

Or maybe an innocent Onex Four would inadvertently supply enough science for them to build a weapon to destroy the good ol' U.S.A and then Uncle Adolph can nonchalantly walk in some sunny morning just in time for church.

Code House Three was located at the end of Vine St. Yep...you got it. Secluded in the Hollywood Hills, Mom's place until she died. It had become run down, now, but intact. The grounds around the house were considerable. Weeds, shrubs and trees tangled around each other. I parked about a block away from 2166 Vine St. I turned the motor off. I hadn't told her yet. "Uh, Miss Winston, I...I've got something—"

"—Fred, please call me Fred." The drugs had pretty much worn off, but I could tell she was still kind of a dizzy dame by nature.

"Fred...I don't know quite how to tell you this but I have some bad news, so better prepare youself. Berguson's been killed. Krieger shot him."

She went white and threw both hands to her face and began to sob. I put my hand over her shoulder, helpless as I usually was when a woman was crying. "I know he was a terrible man in some ways. But I loved him. I found something good in him, something I loved to be with. He made me feel like a woman." Then she got angry. "Why...why did Krieger have to shoot him?"

"You wanna know the truth?"

"Of course," she sobbed

"Because Krieger no longer considered him useful. He had out lived his charming go-between status."

"Oh, God! You take a man's life for that?"

"Yeah, those people do."

Then she fell onto my chest and held me. There I sat with Fredericka Winston on a bright Hollywood morning, wondering what was gonna happen next. If Zorrie Robles was still around, I'll bet she and that crystal ball of hers coulda told me that the past forty-eight hours had been star-crossed with every challenging planetary conjunction possible!

I was concerned about Boots and Eleanor. They had expected my call last night. But I got delayed by a strange underground laboratory and a pre-teenage alien. How would they swallow that story, I wondered. Well, at least I had Fred to back me up. Or had she even seen Onex Four?

I had a key and went to the back. I looked around, spotted no one and took Fred's hand as we climbed up the few creaky stairs to the back door. I no sooner opened it than Boots greeted me with a double-barrel shotgun in my face. "Boots! It's me—and Fredericka." He let down the rifle and immediately Eleanor came running out to embrace her sister. Boots and I pulled them in out of sight.

"So what the hell happened? I'll tell ya, Cable, bein' cooped up with a lovesick woman ain't my idea of fun!"

Then Eleanor ran into my arms and kissed me with all that her body could give and I tried to return with whatever I could. "Tell me...Carlton...is he...is he—?"

"—he's crazy, but he's okay. The krauts are making him work on the other strip to discover its secrets, I'm sure. But your husband is a good man, I sense. He wants to send the alien boy back home."

"So, ya finally saw one of 'em, eh?" Boots asked.

132

Eleanor breathed a sigh of relief. "Thank God he's all right. Now I can rest easier. You understand don't you, Cable?"

"Yeah, sure." I reassured her. Then I warned her. "But don't count on him comin' home singing the *Star Spangled Banner*. He's in deep shit, as all of us are."

Then we all sat for a cup of java and I told my story. At first Boots and Eleanor looked at each other, unbelieving. Hell, I'd have done the same damn thing. By the time I finished and Fred had nodded her sleepy head to confirm it all, we all simply sat there at that little table on a late morning that seemed like any other day. Only it wasn't.

But Boots was sharp. Knowing about the Cape Girardeau incident got those wheels in his head whirling away. "You know, Cable—nothin's ever the way it looks, now is it? I think you should get that klix-strip, or whatever the hell it is, to that alien kid and be done with it. Else how in tarnation will you get them evil pieces of crap off your back without them killin' you first? I wouldn't give a plug nickel for your life just about now."

He took a deep breath, coughed, and spat. "Well one thing we can't complain about. We sure got that excitement I was talkin' about a couple of weeks ago, eh? "

"Yeah, Boots, we got plenty of excitement, the kind people are just dyin' for."

"Well, as I said, I wouldn't give a plug nickel for your skin just about now." Then Boots' offbeat sense of humor got the best of him. "Maybe," he laughed, "we could just hang ya outside with a white flag or some such thing."

133

Eleanor was shocked. "Boots, how can you say such a thing and laugh about it? We're all here. We're all together. We could escape, run and find a place to live until, until the war is over and—"

"—Eleanor...please," I interrupted, "You're thinking with your emotions, and I understand. But you don't get it. There's no escaping these mugs. We're dealing with a whole government here, hell bent on tearing down our way of living, our country, everything we've known. Do you think that they'll think twice about rubbing us out if we're in their way?" I thought for a second. "The *Klix*-strip is the key. If I could get it to this little Onex Four and the other one through a sympathetic Carlton Zelbacher we might somehow get in the clear if we work it right."

Fredericka eagerly volunteered, "I can help, Cable. I can go back to the lab with you and get Carlton to come with us. I know I can."

"Fred!" Eleanor interrupted anxiously. "They'll kill you! They'll kill both of you! There's got to be a better way, somehow. Please!"

"There ain't, babe. Sometimes ya gotta walk into the mouth of the dragon to save the silver chalice. You gotta have the guts to put it all on the line because it's never just about you and me and the neighbor down the street who reads the paper and mows his lawn on Saturday morning. No, it's about preserving a way of life for a whole people. Keeping a remnant of decency intact. And as corrupt as our government is, and as rotten as human nature can sometimes be, still what we have and believe in, is better than nothing. Better than enslavement to a foreign power bent on building a superior race which doesn't happen to include us."

There fell a silence. We were all exhausted. I had to think. But I knew if I didn't sleep, my thoughts would be hazy. And just about now, I needed my thinking to be crystal clear to take that ultimate risk and still come out on top.

Chapter 7

LOVE AND ECSTACY

Eleanor and I crashed on her bed. Neither of us had gotten any sleep the night before. I remember how damn *good* it felt to have this naked woman in my arms once again. She stroked my chest and soon we were both lulled into a much-needed sleep.

When I woke up I could feel her hand lifting and stroking my balls and penis. Her wet womanhood was sliding up and down my leg and her lips were slowly making their way up to mine. What a way for a man to wake up in this cockeyed world, I thought. Soon she was licking me all over and as my body awakened me to the experience of full seduction, fireworks started going off inside my brain as one of her nipples fell into my mouth and I gently kissed and sucked on it.

"Oh, Cable," she was sighing. I couldn't stand being away from you, not having you. You've awakened me, my sexy man, like I've never been awake...like I've never lived before! Take me, Cable, take me...make me yours!"

She rolled over and pulled me up onto her. Her legs spread and then she raised them up around my hips as she welcomed my manhood into her very wet pussy. I sighed and groaned but I couldn't speak. It was like a force that took you over and held you there because it wanted you to go somewhere new, wanted you to experience being inside a keg of dynamite when it went off—wanted you to rip everything away that you've used to shield your phony, safe existence...holding back a bruised heart, not wanting to suffer that pain of loss again.

Eleanor exploded when she came, unable to muffle her responses, she yelled and sighed and shrieked until I was sure the entire neighborhood could hear her. My orgasm into her was like the beginning of my life. I had never felt such a release from the swollen, hard organ I called my cock. My nerve endings transformed into Fourth of July sparklers and everything I was, or thought or felt melted beyond names, words or reason. This incredible woman beneath me surrendered with that complete surrender only a woman in love does and I pumped my hot liquids into her until I thought there wasn't any more and I could die with the last drop of it seeping into her beautiful, swollen womanhood.

For a long time afterward we just lay there clinging to one another, glued by the sweat and juices from our bodies. Neither of us could speak. But I was think-ing...maybe, if you're lucky, something like this might happen once...just once...when it's all green lights down Hollywood Boulevard in the middle of a warm August night. Finally I lifted my head to look at her lovely, young face. I caught her smile through the intensity of her eyes, and we both knew we could not hope to expe-rience this again....'cause you can't hope to hold on to it. Nothing *ever* really happens again in quite the same way twice. It was like a launching off place, the bridge between mortality and immortality. But that scared me, too. It made me wonder, that if I desired her again— which I'm sure I would in about two hours, what would it be like? Could it be expected to measure up....?

"Cable...I love you," she said in a breathy, soft voice. "You don't have to say anything. Just know. That's all. And that's enough for a lifetime."

I don't know what triggered it, but me....tough guy Cable Denning, started to cry. I couldn't control those tears that flowed down onto her breast. Maybe it was because whenever I find myself in the arms of a beautiful, sexy woman who *really* has that true love for me...it's always hard to imagine how a bloke with my beginnings...who still lives mostly in those seedy dark corners of life...could have something like this. A long time ago, I discovered that there is something *beyond ecstasy*. Something almost sacred. But damn! When it *does* come to me, why does it always seem to end in tragedy? Why does the very life I live seem to take it all away? Maybe it was the pain of loss I've buried, gushing up all at once....the women who could love me that way...*dead*....and often at the very hands of the scum I try to beat down. So, do I try to make a go of this? Risk it all happening again? Is this another meteor that can't last and would soon burn up and crash? I couldn't think anymore....I lowered my head between those two beautiful breasts of hers, took both hands and stroked my cheeks with them. There was nothing I could ever say that would even vaguely approach these hours I spent with Eleanor Winston, wife of Dr. Carlton Zelbacher, now the lover of one 42 year-old private dick named Cable Denning.

The Tunnel Turns

"Hey, babe. I know where we're goin'. Right now."

Eleanor smiled at me as she slipped on her dress. "Where?"

"To the Hollywood Dam. You know it? It was built almost 20 years ago now. I remember what a big to-do it was for the Hollywood and Los Angeles area. Local dignitaries were there for the opening day event. Unfortunately Mulholland used so much water from the Owens River to fill it, that the Valley couldn't be used for farming anymore...started some pretty rough 'water wars'. All to build this metropolis that has progressively become a den of corruption. Still it's a great place to walk and think....especially with a beautiful woman by your side." I smiled.

She sidled up to me and whispered in my ear. "You know what? There is so much of us inside of me that my panties are getting all damp from it.

Instinctively I felt up under her dress and grabbed her crotch. Those hot, damp panties were a powerful aphrodisiac and I had to breathe in deep not to throw her back on the bed like a caveman and make love to her again. "Babe...oh, babe," was all I could say.

We greeted Boots and Fredericka who were still at the kitchen table playing cards. "Son-of-a-bitch, Cable, I thought you were killin' the girl in there!"

Eleanor blushed and went over to hug her sister. Fred was very quiet. I knew she was lamenting the loss of Berguson, and I'm pretty sure hearing our moans and groans from the bedroom didn't help. "We're going to take a walk up to the Hollywood dam. Cable says it's close by."

"Yeah, you two, we gotta sit down and talk this thing out when you get back...so get *back*!" Boots asserted.

It was nearing sunset when we arrived at the walk that crossed the dam. Halfway across we stopped and looked at the view of Hollywood below, glowing in the evening's golden light. "Cable," she said in a firm but feminine voice. "You know how helpless a woman in love can be." She looked at me. "That's how I feel. I keep asking myself, where do I fit? So now I'm asking you....where *do* I fit in Cable Denning's life?"

I could hear the pain in her voice. I put my arm around her. "It seems, Toots, after the bliss of love making, we all see the world through those rose-colored glasses. That's where I am just now. I'm filled with you and the brightness of the color blinds me."

"As I am filled with you, my love," she said, tilting her head toward me. "In more ways than one. But I'm not blinded."

Her humor lightened the moment. "We're all tossed into the middle of things that are in the middle of things. Who counted on this?" I kissed her lightly on the lips. "Or this?" I kissed her on her closed eyelids.

She clamped her arms around me as if she would never let me breathe by myself again. "Darling Cable! You always say the right things. You guessed the secret I've always kept in my heart."

"'*Women keep a special corner in their hearts for sins they have never committed.*' At least that's what Cornelius Skinner said."

"And I have committed the greatest sin. It is true. I kept that corner sacred, thinking it would always be a fantasy, something that wouldn't ever come true. It was as if I knew no man could give me that...like some trick of the gods. Zorrie used to say that a man gives love for sex, but that a woman gives sex for love. Is that true for you?"

"I suppose it has been sometimes." I took out a cigarette and lit up.

"Cable, the question still stands: where do I fit? I know you are a loner type of man. And I understand you've had your share of women, but what did they count? You never knew love. Until now, have you?"

"Well, Eleanor, let me level with you. I was thinking about this before, and it wrenched the tears right out of my gut. The truth is....and you know how I feel about truth....that, yes, I've had more than my share of one-night-stands...and strictly-for-sex affairs, but I have also had some pretty serious affairs...the 'thinking about settling down' kind. But they all ended tragically, and I have a lot of pain that gets drudged up sometimes when I am reminded. It's complex, Eleanor. You see, some of the deaths were a result of my kind of business and the scourge I now and again deal with. As you now know, by this thing with Krieger, aliens, intrigue, bizarre science. It's not always marital infidelity that I get hired for. There are some pretty dangerous characters out there and they get obsessed with possessing what they want, and don't care who gets killed on the way. I seem to get thrown in the mixing bowl with that kind of crap. Me being a loner and gun shy, where serious feelings are concerned, is my protection from any repeat performances. But sometimes life throws you a curve ball, and when it comes, ya don't see it comin'. You're looking the other way and suddenly one day a dame walks into your office and when she shakes your hand your toes come up to meet your fingers. And then what?"

"And then what? What do you *want*, Cable?"

I looked into those eyes looking like neon in the setting sun. "It's like this. It's hard to know what you *really* want in life, Eleanor, especially when your life has been like the roller coaster ride mine has. And life has a way of hiding it from you, or experiences cause you to change your mind. It always fools you. You *think* you know what you want, but something goes terribly wrong and then you think, well, maybe I don't really want that anymore....and you go on. And then, I'm not even sure if I can *be* that settling down typa guy now. What if I screw up a good thing, because after all these years I don't know how to change...even if I really want to? Remember what I told you that night across from Zorrie's in that little gin joint? If you're lucky enough for it to come into your life, once it's there you don't know what to do with it."

"So that's it, then? You don't know what to do with me?" Then her voice rose in pitch. "What do you think went on in that bedroom this afternoon? Did you think it was just great sex? Did anything break through that insular barricade you've built around yourself all these years?"

I knew I had the right answer. This time I had to spill it, get it outta my guts so my heart could feel it. "Yeah, babe, I know what happened back there. As much as any two people can, we gave something to each other.

And as far as I can see, we can never take it back. Not now, not today, not tomorrow...not until the fat lady sings."

I took her up into my arms and kissed her so she'd know I meant it. "Cable! Don't ever leave me! I know I sound like a lovesick teenager, but do I have to write it across the sky?"

"No, babe. But it's like I'm two guys. There's this ol' gumshoe who rattles around at forty-two in the same circus ring he's always performed in. Then there's this guy who met this dish. Only this dish makes him believe he can be happy coming home at night to cocktails, soufflés, candlelight, romantic music and great sex. For that guy...it's like a dream...he's passing by the store window, but he doesn't have the money to buy it, so he goes on like he did the day before and the day before that."

She was crying. She looked up and put my face between the palms of her hands. "I say this again, darling. What is it you *want*? Only once, the goddess asks. Come in when the door is open, Cable Denning, for it may never open again. I'm thirty-four and I want your child.

That hit me like a brick! Suddenly my mind was flooded with those lousy memories of 1937—New Year's Eve—Zelda, Cable Jr., little Nan. I had decided to grab that chance at home and family and everything that goes with it. That night, Zelda and Nan were mysteriously abducted....gone....just like that! I failed miserably alone as a father for Cable, Jr. Is there a chance I could make it work—here and now—with Eleanor?

Can't tell her about all that now....another time....another place.

Eleanor, sensing my delay, slowly put her arms around my waist and pressed her head into my chest. "You know, Cable, we may have done just that this afternoon....conceived a child. Do you know how incredibly delicious that feels?"

"I dunno. Sounds pretty crazy."

"Then let the two of us be crazy...and in love...and happy...and devoted parents who live happily ever after. What's wrong with that? I'm not afraid to grow old with you. Can't we spend the rest of our lives thinking only about things we love?"

What *was* wrong with that? I thought, feeling myself losing ground fast. So much was pouring into me at the same time. It was like I was standing underneath the dam and suddenly it broke and I was drowning in the water. It was slamming me down, pushing me up, and floating me away. Then I heard myself say, "Alright. Let me say this while I have the guts to say it. Let's get this whole mess straightened out with the stupid strip, Carlton and Krieger. Okay? Then, I know a place in a little gambling town named Reno where two people can get hitched and say to hell with all the rest of it."

"Oh, Cable!" she sighed and held me to her. Then she grew serious. "Let's skip the first part of it. Let's just go. Now."

"What about your husband?"

"I left him years ago. I told you he was never for me. Now he's going to die. I know it, I can feel it."

"And Boots and Fred?"

"We'll take them with us. Please, Cable, hear me!"

"If we don't get that damn strip to them, they'll kill us all, Eleanor."

"They'll kill us anyway, even if we do deliver that terrible alien thing. Fred tells me these guys are monsters, worse than the aliens they're protecting. Where's the strip now?

"Under the rug on the passenger side of my coupe."

"Oh, God. That scares me just thinking about it."

We remained silent as we walked hand-in-hand back to the Vine Street house. It seemed strange…there were no lights on. I told Eleanor to wait but she didn't want to be left alone. We approached the front door this time. I had learned an old Indian trick by rolling silently up the eight or ten stairs to the large front porch. Eleanor ducked behind a large bush below the porch out of sight. I put my ear to the door. Suddenly Krieger's two big goons stepped out of the dark shadows and grabbed me. I yelled for Eleanor to run but she ran up the stairs to help me and they subdued both of us.

They dragged us inside, and a lamp went on in the west corner of the living room. "Such a pleasure, Mr. Denning. Now I am *your* guest—and *I* have the gun," Anton Krieger remarked in that voice of his.

"What happened to the twenty-four hours, Krieger? Can't you count?"

"Oh, I forgot to tell you. One of my secret passions is not keeping my word. Especially when the art of surprise is an option. Moral codes are such a waste of time."

"You worm! I knew I shoulda wiped you out at Forest Lawn and left you with all the other maggots! But

I'm not a cold-blooded murderer. Where are Boots and Fredericka?"

"Do you mean are they dead yet?"

"Yeah, something like that." I glanced over at Eleanor. She was trembling, her eyes glued to me as if she was waiting for some signal from me. But one of the goons had a death-grip on her arm and held her in place.

"Well, now, they are just *fine*—tied up in your tussled bedroom awaiting you. You see, Mr. Denning, I'm rather into *mass* executions." He looked Eleanor over from head to toe. "My, my, your lady friend is such a...a...what do you call it in your English slang?"

"Dish...you piece of shit."

"Yes. Dish. I like the term. Quaint." He reached over to a bowl of pecan nuts. "I hope you'll forgive my manners for not asking. But I do love pecans. The sweetness sits tastefully on the tongue, you know."

"Okay, you kraut sewer rat. What now in that sick brain of yours?"

"Cable...please don't goad him! He'll kill you!" Eleanor shouted.

"Why thank you, Eleanor Winston. At least one of you is sticking up for me." Then he glowered at me, still with a smile. "She's right, you know. Perverse insults seem to accumulate in my head. Do you recall, Mr. Denning, our conversation about genius in an unwell personality? Well, you are about to witness the unwell personality part of my rather complex makeup. It's the one that delights in the presence of pain, and is intrigued with the sight of death...or dying...whichever comes first."

"Give me one crack at you, Krieger. Just one. I won't fail this time. Somehow, vermin like you gives me the motivation to do it!"

"How colorful! You Americans do love your slang now, don't you?" Then he grew very serious. "Before I can kill you without remorse, Mr. Denning, we are still unresolved in the matter of the *Klix*-strip. But fret not. I have a plan. I shall kill off...is that the right movie gangster phrase? Anyway, I shall shoot right before your eyes one by one, your dear friends until you give me the strip."

"And after you kill everyone, Krieger, and ya still don't have the strip, then what? Are ya gonna start all over again and find another group of people to kill?"

"Ah, you are so obnoxious and resistant, Mr. Denning. Perhaps it is best to torture you before your friends. We can start by ripping away your male organs. That's also one of my favorites, coming in somewhere between pain and death."

Eleanor shrieked, " Oh my God, Cable...!

"Torture *is* painful, you idiot!" I shouted at the insolent Kraut. "And what will you gain when I lose consciousness?"

"Good question. I don't know. We still won't know where the *Klix*-strip is, will we?"

I was thinking fast, trying to bluff him. "You see, you're stupid, you blithering kraut, my pain threshold is rather low. So it wouldn't do you much good to rip out my family jewels. And my guess is, that you don't even have any of your own." Krieger started up from his seat toward me. Then he thought better of it and sat back down. He thought for a moment. "You do not seem to

147

fear dying, Mr. Denning. While that may appear brave, with my many methods of torture, all of that is moot. For we have little, tiny ways of inducing pain *without* you passing out. Dammil!" He called over the one goon who wasn't holding Eleanor in place. "Fetch Mr. Blake and the charming Fredericka. Every fine deed needs witnesses, you know."

"Please! Let him go! I know where the strip is!" Eleanor blurted out. I could not believe she would implicate herself...or worse yet, give away the location of the strip in my coupe.

Krieger seemed genuinely surprised. "My dear, how good of you to come forth with that information. But if you think it will save your lover man...isn't that what the Billie Holiday song says? *Lover Man?* I like American blues and jazz...anyway, you will be mistaken if you think it will help him, young woman." He fidgeted with the gun in his hand, moving it back and forth from palm to palm nervously. He glanced up to see one of his goons bring in Boots and Fred. That was all the time I needed to streak across the room and lunge at Krieger, bringing him to the floor just as he fired his weapon into the ceiling. He was out of shape and I wrestled the gun from his hand in a flash and then put it to his head. The shocked little weasel of a man began to tremble.

"Now...you two goons freeze. You!" I pointed to the one who held Eleanor. "Release her or you're dead." He dropped her arm. "Yeah! Both of you, hands up over your heads." Just then one of them tried to make a break for the door. I wasn't too familiar with a Luger but I fired and splattered his brains against the front door anyway. He fell— a little spasm and then he was dead. I shoved Krieger up to sit on the floor leaning against the chair he was sitting in earlier. The other goon who had come out with Boots and Fred stood trembling, his hands high.

Eleanor came running over to me. "Careful, babe. Not too close. We've got the snakes cornered, but now we've gotta dispose of 'em. You made a big mistake, Krieger. You didn't arm your Deutsche wrestlers. You thought German brawn was enough to conquer American know-how, didn't you, you fucking scum!"

"God, Cable Denning, I love you…I've never seen…"

"Save it, babe. We've got some fast thinking to do. Boots, get your gun and come on over and tie this one up while I take care of Mr. Germany, Class of '41 here."

"Ich muss meine arme ruhen—oder Ich werde meine hose nass!"

"What's he saying, Krieger?"

The shocked little man on the floor looked up at me disgustingly. "He says if you don't let him take his arms down he shall…shall urinate in his pants."

"Oh." So I simply took the back of the Luger and knocked him cold. Now his arms were down. "Tie him up, Boots."

Boots did as I asked and then he and Fred came over and joined Eleanor in hugging a piece of me. "Damn, boy!" Boots said. "That's some of the best damn fearless action I've witnessed in a long, long time. Dammit, Cable, you're one hell of a cop!"

"Thank you, again," Fred said as she kissed me. Eleanor took Fred into the kitchen to prepare some coffee.

"Fill mine with gin gypsy!" I yelled.

I looked down at Krieger. "You know, you weaselly son-of-a-bitch, the young psychic you beat up and eventually killed would've said you and I have a *karmic* relationship. One of us owes the other something, Krieger. What do you think?"

But Krieger was silent for a change.

Eleanor came out and gave me a cup of gin with some coffee and liqueur in it. "Boots tells me that this was your mother's place. It just stays empty most of the time?"

"Uh....yeah, it's been more or less empty for about 5 years now...except I occasionally come up and plop down in a chair and drift down memory lane listening to Bing Crosby sing *Black Moon- light*, or Jolsen croon *Sonny Boy*." I reached for the phone. "Police headquarters, Central Division, downtown Los Angeles. Lieutenant Keith, please." I waited at the other end as Eleanor held my arm. Damn, that felt good. I didn't show it then, but I was pretty shaken up by the events of the past hour or so. "Yeah, operator, then get me the 77th Division Los Angeles Police Department, thanks."

Soon a voice came over the other end. "Homicide. Keith"

"Lieutenant? Cable Denning here. This time I've got three thugs for you. One's pretty dead with his brains on the inside of my mother's front door. The other two," I said, glancing over at Krieger tied up on the floor, "are definitely for pick-up"

"That's a mouthful, Denning. You've been a busy boy. Don't move. I'll be right there."

A half hour later Lester Keith was at the door with a somewhat undesirable tag-along, one Carmine Williamson, a tough ex-thug turned cop some years back. We scooted the dead oaf's body over so we could open the door but left the spattered entrails for the Coroner's office. Keith came in and looked around. He asked for Krieger's Luger and told us he couldn't hold the two men long because they weren't American citizens.

"Whatta ya mean, Keith, I break my balls to bring these guys down and you wanna let 'em go?" I sputtered, quite perturbed.

"Not in my jurisdiction. I have to turn them over to the Feds, Denning. This being wartime and all, I wouldn't be surprised if they might be here illegally doing something they shouldn't. By the way, what else do you know about them?"

I had to keep quiet about some things, at least until I decided the fate of the *Klix*-strip. Or did it have a mind of its own? "They were wrapped up in a plot to extort Miss Fredericka Winston here. Krieger, the little rodent in the corner, killed her one-time boyfriend Berguson in cold-blood. Now, *that* I witnessed."

"Where was that?"

"Forest Lawn."

"Appropriate. So let me get it straight." His speech was halting as he ticked off the facts. "You got involved in this case originally through... Miss Winston here having to do with... finding Berguson. But it became more complicated. A second Miss Winston got involved to help her sister. But Berguson was... blackmailing the first sister and sent you to deliver an envelope of cash to an address on... Lanterman Terrace where no one lived. You arrive to deliver the envelope. The door's open. You go in a dark room and someone, presumably;

151

Berguson, saps you on the head and you're out for hours. When you come to you don't have the envelope but you've a big lump on your skull...and no Berguson, right?"

"Yep. Right as rain so fair, Lieutenant," I said.

"Now the... first Miss Winston disappears and the... second Miss Winston, Eleanor, now hires you to find *her*. Your first visit for clues takes you to... the now-deceased Madam Zorrie Robles. How am I doing?"

"That sounds pretty accurate, Lieutenant Keith," Eleanor replied, knowing we were leaving Carlton Zelbacher out of the equation. "She warned us that Fred's...Fredericka's...kidnappers were treacherous and trouble was right behind them."

"There's still something missing here, if you don't mind my saying so. Why would they work over your friend, Zorrie Robles, and eventually kill her, when all you did was visit her for a psychic reading?"

Eleanor glanced at me and I back at her. "There was something else they wanted," I chimed in. "Fredericka had a very precious jeweled necklace. It was worth a couple hundred grand. She hid it for safe keeping just before she was kidnapped and maybe, uh, well maybe..."

"They thought I had given the necklace to my sister to give to Zorrie Robles, whom I also knew," Fredericka lied to the cops. "Who knows what those horrible men think?"

I shot a quick glance over to the sly, carefully attentive Krieger. He kept shut. He knew he had to. He was in big trouble.

"So...did you give the neck piece to Miss Robles?"

"No. I hid it in my house."

"I see. Well, that's all for now. Nobody leaves town. Right? We'll call the Coroner for the meat wagon...the second this month on your behalf, Denning...and perhaps you can send over a maid to clean up the place after we leave."

"Don't steal the candelabras, Lieutenant", I snickered at Keith. "My mother was partial to them..."

The four of us stayed in a hotel that night. It had been a hell of a day. Yet when Eleanor slipped into bed with me and our smells emanated from her body, I was filled with desire again and again for her. Sometime during the early hours of the morning she had gone to the bathroom. When she returned she found me staring up at the ceiling. I was thinking a thousand things, spinning out of control. And for me not to be in control of my life, felt like whatever it was that helped me keep my sanity.....was slipping. "Penny for your thoughts," she whispered.

I held out my arm and she cuddled into it. "I was just thinkin' how babes like you are a dame-a-dozen," I joked. "And how easy you were to be suckered here into this hotel room with me...this traveling salesman from Vermont."

She giggled. "You know, I never saw anyone take such command of a situation like you did today, Cable. I was frightened to death for both of us. Yet you stood up against that horrible little man and his henchmen...and you won."

"We were lucky the two apes didn't have rods in their pockets. I almost dropped my teeth when you told Krieger you knew where the *strip* was."

"It bought us the right amount of time for you to catch him off guard and pounce, didn't it?"

"Come 'ere, you." I drew her to me and kissed her. We sailed slowly out of conversation into the land of sleep.

I hadn't been to my office in a while, so I sent Eleanor, Fred and Boots over to the Winston place where they could change clothes and freshen up. As long as Krieger was under lock and key I figured it was safe enough. I was still wearing the same smelly old clothes I was wearing on Wednesday. I was delighted to find Ida Latney sitting at my desk sorting out my mail. She got up as soon as she saw me enter. "Oh, Mr. Denning! You didn't tell me you were coming in."

"You didn't tell me *you* were coming in…."

"How could I? I didn't know where you were. But I still have the key you gave me in January."

I surveyed the room. "I owe you some money and lunch, young lady. Thanks for cleaning up and putting me up the other night. It was a life saver….literally."

"You're welcome, Mr. Denning. I threw out all the empty liquor bottles, emptied the ashtrays, swept the floor, dusted the shelves, cleaned your bathroom, took in and sorted the mail."

"Ida, you are a miracle worker. Yep…you are going to make some lucky young man a good wife."

"I wish. All the guys are signing up to go to war," she complained. "Pretty soon there won't be any eligible men left in Los Angeles."

"Well, I wouldn't worry about that. You've always got me, Ida," I kidded her. "And I'm going to clean up right now and change clothes. So… uh…I'll go over the mail later. If anyone calls, take a message and tell 'em I'm not here yet."

"Yes, sir."

I got into the bathroom and ran the hot water. I picked my old second-class razor off the shelf and dropped it on the floor. But when I bent down to pick it up, a terrible pain shot through my hip and I yelled.

In a flash Ida was at my side. "What is it, Mr. Denning?"

"Aggh! Oh! I've got some kinda cramp in my hip…I need to sit down on the bed a minute."

She grabbed an arm and helped me over to the bed. "Lie down, if you can. My dad used to get things like this. Here, let me massage it for you." I stripped my shirt off, pulled my trousers down a bit and she dug her magic hands into my flesh. It felt damn good. This petite little thing was strong. After a while, I began to feel Ida's touch was doing more than I had anticipated. When a man is turned on from one woman, sometimes it carries over to any fair damsel who happens to accidently touch the right places. Ida Latney was doing just that right then.

"Uuh…I think that's swell for now, Ida. Thanks. It feels a lot better."

There was a knock at the door and a shout. "Mailman! Package for you, Mr. Denning!" At the same time the phone rang and Ida went to answer it as I got up and pulled my shirt on.

"Cable Denning, Private Investigator's office," Ida announced in a business-like clear tone. "Oh, yes, just a moment please." She got up and came in to the bedroom. "It's a Lieutenant Lester Keith, Mr. Denning."

I ambled to the phone and picked it up, my hip still twitching a bit. "Yeah, Lieutenant, Cable here...."

"I've done all I can to keep Krieger and his gorilla behind bars, but the FBI came and hauled them out this morning."

"Well, you told me that might happen. What'd you find out about Krieger and do the Feds know he's murdered two people we know of already?"

"Well, there are no traces, no records, no fingerprints, no nothin'. He don't exist. I think that's the common modus operendi with spies, though."

"What about that big black Lincoln he was driving? Who's it registered to?"

"Let me see...one Maya Stoldthedder, 4600 Los Feliz Boulevard, apt. 201."

"Thanks, Lester Keith, I owe you one."

"You owe me a lot. As far as I'm concerned, *you* should be behind bars. Good bye, Denning. Hope I don't see you too soon."

I hung up, debating whether I should call Eleanor and the others and tell them more than likely Krieger would be on the loose again very soon. But maybe, just maybe, the FBI would find enough on that sick son-of-a-bitch to hold him a while. At least one could hope justice would reign true somewhere inside those inner sanctums of law enforcement and investigation.

Ida had stacked the incoming mail and the small package on my desk and then went about other things she had been instructed to do under my tutelage. Most of the mail turned out to be unpaid bills, advertisements and letters from prospective clients. The small package was filled with photographs of some middle-aged man pursuing a teenager at the beach. The note inside read, *'How many years in prison can my husband serve from chasing around a fourteen year-old in Santa Monica? He is a district judge. Please call, Jo Ann, at HO-6511.'* I snickered to myself when I read the note. Seemed no one was exempt from sexual impulse, including me.

"Ida, let me ask you a question," I said, summoning the pretty young woman. I handed her the note. "What would you do? Would you take this case...and consider what laws are being broken here?"

Ida studied the photos. "Well, she is awfully pretty. And quite developed for her age. But he seems too old for her. Plus, I don't know the law, but I've heard that penalties for harassing under-aged children are becoming much more strict."

"Yeah, especially if he touches her, it could be statutory rape. That's a year or two in the slammer, if he's convicted."

"Oh, dear...and he's a judge? He should know better."

"You can be sure he does know better, Miss Latney. But the sexual drives in men and women often cause them to cross that thin line leading to criminal activity. After all, that's how our business here survives."

"There was a friend of my Dad's who tried once to put his hand under my dress when I was about eleven."

"And what did you do, Ida?"

157

"I took his hand , slapped it, and told him I'd tell my Dad if he ever got close to me again." She began to walk away. "So he never bothered me again."

"So as an adult young woman, what do ya think of men?"

"I love men. I've never been..." She flushed, looking away from me. "Been intimate with a man outside of kissing and some feeling around, you know. My mother was very strict and she still warns me about all the trouble women can get into with men. I guess she got pregnant with me and married my Dad."

"Yep, that's the way a lot of us get here, Ida. Don't take it personally."

" Oh, I don't. But I sure would like to meet some man to ...." In her embarrassment her voice trailed off. Then, she found her words again. "... After all, I'm going to be *thirty* pretty soon."

"Uh, uh! I think we'd better stop right there, Ida. Sorry, it was none of my business," I said....rather ashamed I'd let it go that far. "How about a late lunch? I owe you at least that."

"That would be wonderful, Mr. Denning."

Before Ida and I left for lunch I decided to call Eleanor and tell her to be wary, for the monster may be loosed from his cage sooner than we thought. She was distressed, wanted to know when I'd be home and promised to tell the others.

We went to a little joint on Hollywood Blvd. They had good food, imported beer, wine and a waitress that looked like Mae West at 20.

"What 'cha want, guys?" Our waitress's accent drawled with a cross between New York and Memphis.

We sat in a small booth next to a window looking out onto the true 'Boulevard of Broken Dreams'.

I looked up at the buxom babe with a half-smile. "Uh...well, we don't know yet. Haven't really looked at the menu."

She groaned with disdain. "Yeah, just like a man. Don't know if he wants dessert or the main course."

Now I knew she was playing the May West role, hoping some movie mogul might be having lunch here one day and discover her.

Ida and I smiled at each other and then we ordered. I looked across at Ida. Although she had worked for me on and off for over two years, I never really stopped long enough to find out what she was really like.

"So, tell me, Ida. Did you ever wanna act or be in the movies?"

"No. Too wild for me. I'd just like to meet someone and settle down, maybe have a child or two. I'm not ambitious. Not like my roommate, Dorrie...who's beautiful and very aggressive with men. Especially men in power like movie moguls and producers and the like."

"Oh, I see."

"But she never gets the parts. I don't know..."

"Why do you think that is...isn't she talented enough?"

"No, that's not it. There are just so *many* pretty girls in Hollywood. Plus I think she goes to bed with some of the casting directors. She had to have an abortion a few months ago." Ida looked up at me from her sandwich.

I was learning a lot. I mean, not a lot I didn't already know. But the dog-eat-dog world of Hollywood was one part art and talent and one part sex machine. The Dorries of the world came in droves to get discovered long before the 1920's, before voices came with the film. Countless young broads got screwed repeatedly until it finally dawned on them it wasn't gonna be who you slept with or who *said* they could grant favors promised, that was going to get these gals with starry eyes and eager bodies where they wanted to go. Rarely, a Davis, Crawford, Barrymore, Tierney and the like came along who could make it on pure talent. But it did happen now and then I supposed. Unless....

"So, what do *you* want, Mr. Denning? I mean, I know you've been a private investigator for a long time. But don't you ever get lonely? Don't you ever want to come home to someone with a just-cooked dinner on the table and a warm bed where someone holds you all night?"

Eleanor's image popped into my head like a goddess summoning me to the temple. "Yeah, Ida, I do. But ya know the life of a gumshoe. My hours are all screwed up. Plus it's dangerous work sometimes. This life-style of mine has already brought about tragedy. Like this thing I'm tangled up in right now. I could end up in a garbage can in some dark alley somewhere....or bring that someone to harm just from being with me....and that's not very good grounds for a serious future.

I hit a soft spot. Ida's eyes welled with tears. "Don't say that, Mr. Denning. Please." Then she reached her hand across the little table and held my wrist. "I know you think I'm really young and immature, compared to your life and world. But sometimes simple is wonderful. Maybe it's the best. I don't think I'm too young for you. Oh dear. Now I've said it, haven't I?" She looked down and swallowed hard. "I'm embarrassed and I'll never speak of this again. Just know, if you ever change your mind about someone…"

"That's the best proposal I've ever had, Ida." I didn't want to crush the young thing down. She deserved to be heard because probably so few men ever took that extra sip on their beer to listen to her. "But I've gotta be on the level with you. Recently, I met someone that I'm having that very struggle inside about. As a matter of fact it's this case I'm on that threw us together." She drew her hand back and settled both of them on her lap. The disappointment was obvious in Ida's eyes. But soon she perked up and smiled at me. "Well, maybe it's best that way. And I'm happy for you. And now I can work for you without thinking about that day when you might get lonely and reach for me."

"Yeah, Ida, you're savin' yourself from a lotta heartache. Believe me, I'm no easy bloke to be around, kid. You see how I live, like some caveman. But I'm flattered you would consider a broken down ol' dick who's twelve years your senior."

"Thank you, Mr. Denning. I love honesty. I think that's why I've cared about you. Because you care about honesty."

I smiled across the table at her and held my hands palm-open. She placed her hands trustingly in mine. "Well, let's go now, Ida. Here." I took out a ten-spot and handed it to her. "You do good work. And thanks for the massage."

She looked at the money and then at me. "Ten dollars! Thank you. Anytime, Mr. Denning. When do you want me next?"

"Well, come back next Wednesday. Use your key. Come late. Don't wait much longer than after dark. If I don't phone by 9:00 p.m., go home."

"Alright."

Ida left to use the lady's room. I waited outside. What kind of a chance would a nice mid-western gal like her have in this cockeyed world? Maybe someday she'd find someone like her, clean, straight with a good heart. And maybe then she'd know love. Ida came back out and we started for her place.

"Is there some place I can reach you?"

"I won't know until that day. If there is, I'll call and give you a number. If Lieutenant Keith calls, tell him I'm in town but not available until Thursday. Got it?"

"Okay....got it, Mr. Denning." We didn't speak much after that, until we said good night, and I headed down towards my office.

In the midst of all the happiness I'd known lately, why was I so damned depressed? There was an envelope without a postmark on the front mat to my office. I picked it up. No return address, either. I entered and plopped down into my still comfy chair. I poured a fat gin and lit up a Lucky Strike. I opened the envelope. It was Eleanor's writing.

My Dearest Darling,

How difficult it is to be without you. The hours go by like days, no matter how I try to fill them. Sometimes, when I collect my thoughts and feelings, I can say best who I am when I am with you. Nothing compares. Ever.

I had to take a bath today. When I washed you off my body, my heart hurt a little. All I could do was hope you'll

162

fill me again and again with your beautiful essence and make me dance inside all day. I now think this is part of a woman's joy. Having a mate she's truly in love with and hoping with all that is womanly in her, that he may impregnate her one day.

It is my prayer, Cable, that in some beautiful moment, your heart will burst open enough for you to know how much you are loved. For if one keeps passing by when true love is offered, then it could be lost forever.

As I write, I realize you have been a wish inside me for most of my life. Only I didn't know it. But I want you to know it now. Forgive my awkwardness with words. But a song probably says it best for me, my love:

'I could cry salty tears. Where have I been all these years?

Little, wow. Tell me now. How long has this been going on?

There were chills up my spine and some thrills I can't define.

Listen, sweet. I repeat. How long has this been going on?

I feel that I could melt, into Heaven I'm hurled!

I know how Columbus felt finding another world!

Kiss me once, then once more. What a dunce I was before!

What a break! For Heaven's sake...

How long has this been going on?'

My darling, this is only the first page of my love song to you, come home when you can!

Your passionately, ever-loving Eleanor

I folded the note. My whole body just sat there like a passive lump, my eyes fixed on Eleanor's last words. When a man like me receives something priceless like this, he wonders who was it addressed to really? What living man could possibly be worthy of such a love? No matter how deep I might reach inside myself, would I ever live up to her image of me? I knew the Gershwin song. It was slow and sexy. Just like her. I tucked the letter back in its envelope. My cigarette had burned down, so I lit up again. This time I took a deep drag and washed it down with a swallow of gin, maybe trying to numb myself a little.

I was looking at my scratch pad and scanned the name and address of the dame who owned Krieger's bloodstained Lincoln. Maya Stoldthedder, 4600 Los Feliz Blvd., Apt. #201. Maybe that was the first place to look for a clue and I needed the diversion.

Chapter 8

JAZZ ME SOME BLUES

It was one of those fancy doorbells that rang several tones before it was finished.

"Ya? Who is it?" a very firm woman's voice demanded.

"I'm the guy who saw Krieger shoot Berguson in the back seat of your car," I answered.

Immediately the door opened and a very tightly wrapped middle-aged woman with thick hair touched with a little silver and wide, fierce blue-eyes appeared. "You should not announce such tings! You never know who hears. It is against de rules."

"Oh, yes, the rules. I forgot how many bendable rules you Huns have."

"I am no Hun, dummkopf! I am an Austrian, like Herr Zimmer-Kleiber."

"Who? Now that's a new name to me, lady."

"Krieger's his American name."

"Doesn't sound very American to me."

"I mean…vell, you know vat I mean!"

Actually, the woman was quite attractive with a kind of Marlene Dietrich sound to her voice. Kinda low and sexy. "Well, I won't be staying long. My name is Cable Denning. I'm the guy who got mixed up in this mess and rode in your car out to Trancas Beach to see you-know-who-and-you-know-what."

"I am Maya Stoldthedder. My real name. At least, sit down for a moment, Herr Denning. I hate standing up ven I am undressing someone."

165

"That's *a*-dressing someone, Miss Stoldthedder."

"Ya. Vatever you say, den. You Americans have such a bastard of a language. How do you write und spell correctly? You should have stricter rules."

"Oh, yeah, the rules again. Well, anyway, where is your car now, if you don't mind me asking?"

"In de repair shop."

"I assume you know it is probably pretty mussed up, especially with Berguson's blood all over the back seat."

"See? I vas reluctant to loan mein auto to Zimmer-Kleiber. Now he has me in de trouble vith de police. Dey came here also."

"Yes, so I've been informed. But where is your friend Zimmer-Kleiber, alias Krieger?"

"In jail, I hope. But he is *not* my friend. De Austrian pro-counsel requested dat I loan him mein auto for a few days. May I offer you a varm German beer? It is very much de best."

"Ah, no thanks, Miss...Miss..."

"Maya, call me Maya. It becomes easier that way."

"Okay, Maya. You do know Krieger is very dangerous, not to mention psychopathic, don't you?"

"Ya, I know he's crazy and he has been kaput in his head since vay back when he vas a child. You know de kind, brilliant but empty inside."

"Yeah. I know the kind. That was sorta my take, but you can add not even a whit of *conscience* to that."

She looked me over. "You become pretty handsome for a gummy-who, or..."

"Gumshoe. That's a nickname for a private dick."

"Vat? Private who? Dat's embarrassing since ve hardly know each odder, Herr Denning."

I laughed inside at this inadvertently comical lady. "No, no, Maya. All it means is private investigator."

She turned the word around on her tongue. "Inwestigator.... oh. Vell, dat's different. So vat to you vant from me, Herr Cable?"

"Herr...Mr. Denning, Cable Denning."

"Vatever you say, den. I got to have a drink. Vant a drink?"

"We've already been through that, Maya. I don't like warm beer. Americans don't drink much warm beer."

"Too bad. It's better for you. Cold beer, it is unhealthy."

"I need to know where Krieger is going to show up next. I've got a gut feeling the Feds are not gonna keep him long. Are you a citizen?"

"Ya! Ya! I *am* a citizen! Humph! I work hard for the German Embassy here in Los Angeles."

Now I was beginning to see the connection. Maya was set up, a dupe, like so many that Krieger and his gang had used as a means to accomplish their ends. "I'm afraid you can't help me beyond what you've told me. Thank you..."

She ran over to me with that warm beer in her hand. "But I *can* help you, Herr Denning. I don't vant to be part of dis dirty ting Zimmer-Kleiber is involved in!" She shoved the mug under my chin. "Here, nice man, take a zip."

I tried the stuff and it wasn't so bad. Just not my cup of tea. "So how can you help me? I don't see..."

"I know vat Zimmer-Kleiber killed people for...he disobeyed de *rules* und went out of de authority of de *Lichter Grabstätte*."

Phew! That sounded like another can of worms to me. "And what is that, if I may ask?"

"I cannot be sure. But they are rich und secret. Dey knew you had vun of der stolen pieces from der space wreck. I intercepted dat message by accident from der decoder at work. Dat's when dey decided to loan mein auto to Zimmer-Kleiber."

Now it hit me and sweat began forming on my forehead. "I have one suggestion, Maya. Pack your bags and get out of here, now, tonight and never come back. Do you understand that?"

She threw her hands in the air. "But vhy?"

"Don't you understand that you know too much?"

"But who vill feed my exotic fish?" she inquired as she ran toward me and grabbed my arm. "Please take me mit you! I can cook, sew, I am intelligent company...und for no extra...perhaps I can be a real...freundin to you."

I was trying to be polite. "Look, Maya, thanks for the offer. But I've got a loaded plate here...and you'd be just one more thing I couldn't deal with. You see, it's like this. I know so little about what's at the bottom of all the crap that's going on here. And your Zimmer-Kleiber is the triggering mechanism."

"Den I vill leave. I like you, Herr Denning. How about a little 'smooch' before you go, big boy?"

We both laughed as I made for the door. I thanked Maya Stoldthedder and bade her good-bye as fast as I could. I definitely had to come up for air.

Whenever I felt the world falling in around me, there was only one place in this nutso city I could go. It was my hiding cave, in the form of a nightclub—the

Blue Gardenia was the kind of place you stepped down into, and once inside the smoke was blue, the spotlight a dirty yellow and the inhabitants—escapees from every zoo that life offered. Charlie Granelli played a blow sax that was outta this world. He had a stand-up bass player who looked like Louie Armstrong and his drummer, Felix the Helix Davidson, grooved on the drums. But it was the combination of Charlie and his great Negro piano player, Tocuni Reese, that gave you those chills up the spine and made you remember what real jazz and blues were all about.

I walked in about 10:30 after I called Eleanor and told her I was going down for air. She didn't understand that, but only a night denizen like me could drag his way into a nightclub like the *Blue Gardenia* and emerge healed from the all the woes that beset the world.

The place was jammed and noisy, but that's how I liked it. All those voices and sounds were like hearing children in a playground on Saturday morning. "Hey there, Cable Denning! Man...where your chops been hangin' lately?" Tocuni Reese greeted me as I walked up to his piano. I nodded to the rest of the guys as they were playing some drippy ballad that was a cross between *Sugar Blues* and *My Chinatown*.

"Well....I've been to London to visit the bombs," I said. He laughed and kept playing.

Then in back of me I heard a familiar voice from out of my past. "Hey, handsome P.I. I haven't heard *that* voice for a while." I turned around and it was June Maye. I always remembered her name because it simply had the months reversed. Just add the 'e'. She was

169

bleached blonde now, maybe middle-thirties, good looking little gal with a great figure. She had beautiful gray eyes and the kind of smile you wanna wake up to at the breakfast table. A few years earlier June Maye and I had a hot thing going. I was captivated by her singing and she was intrigued with the unsolvable me. We made sure that we kept love out of the equation. Yeah....and we got into some pretty bad stuff and spiraled down so low, that we didn't care what we were becoming. But I sure had a soft spot for the dame. She introduced me to the Gershwin brothers' *How Long Has This Been Going On?* And floored me. The very same song Eleanor had quoted the lyrics to in her note to me this very day! How can life have so many ironies?

When June sang it, I was instantly transported. It was like a memory I didn't remember having, but it was stuck inside of me there, tugging and pulling at my guts until the tears came.

"June!" I said. I went up and hugged her. "It's great to see you! You know me....the stench got pretty bad out there, so I had to come back down for air...and here *you* are! I'm really glad to see that you're back up there on the stage where you belong. Will you sing for me?" I could tell she'd been drinking and her speech slurred a bit.

"Sure. What?"

"You know what."

There was a slight trace of pain on her face and her eyes misted. "Sure, Cable, I'm a glutton for punishment, aren't I? I'm still picking out pieces of shrapnel from that last ride with you.

"I'm sorry, kid..."

"Yeah, I know, Cable.....sorry for what?" she asked me.

Her eyes were misty. I took out my handkerchief and dabbed her eyes. "Well, lots of water under the bridge, kid. I dunno, June...whatta ya say after ya say you're sorry?"

"That's a song, too, Cable," she said with that half-smile. She walked away and waded through the crowded tables until she was on the tiny stage with that terrible dirty yellow spot light turning her nice green dress into something dreadful. But when Granelli and Tocuni started up, I found one seat at the bar, ordered a honeyed whiskey in a snifter of hot water and turned to look at June. I choked up on the first six notes.

I could cry salty tears. Where have I been all these years?

Little, wow. Tell me now. How long has this been going on?

There were chills up my spin and some thrills I can't define.

Listen, sweet. I repeat. How long has this been going on?

When she finished singing she was crying and the crowd went wild. I had melted back down to a puddle of salt water on a forgotten floor somewhere in the dark. What was it in her that she wouldn't let out....except when she sang? Maybe she and I were just too much alike....both content to live behind that wall against too much serious emotional involvement. Maybe Eleanor was a reminder from the cosmos, that some kind of

171

mysterious synergy exists in this cockeyed universe and I was being banged over the head with it. But there were always gonna be casualties along the way.

June came over to my stool. "Babe, look here..." I showed her my wet eyes. "You see, you still have the same effect on me."

"Yeah, you and twenty other guys in here. It's a sentimental soaker, Cable, that's all. But thanks for the compliment." Then she walked away toward a small table in a dark corner of the joint. Someone was waiting for her.

I was disappointed she felt that way about the great tune. Or maybe that was just June putting up that wall again. I remembered she was a bit bitter when I pulled out of the relationship. She thought it was a good match, especially the hours we kept, the drinking we'd do...and she smoked as much as I did! She was great in the bedroom, too. It was a strange thing. Sometimes after a while with a babe, you wake up lonely one morning. Then you know it's over. But June and I were so full of drugs and booze that we didn't know the difference...but there was still a piece missing with June. I didn't feel that with Eleanor. It was all there.

By the time the boys in the band finished with a dynamite version of *Life Is Just a Bowl of Cherries* and June reprised with *Body and Soul*, I was healed. The *Blue Gardenia* had done its magic. I was ready to go, so I said good-night to the band and went over to June, who was sitting with a handsome, younger man. "June, I just want ya to know the way you do a song.....still grabs me, Doll. So, as always kid, until the next time..." I tipped my hat to her.

She was pretty lit by now. "Sure...you're okay, Kindle...uh...I...I mean Cable. This is Joseph. He's a big fan, too, aren't you, Joseph?" The two of us nodded at each other. "Cable here...and I...once had a wild and torrid love affair. He took this gal while she was young and pretty and made her into...into—a hell of a singer! Only heartbreak does that to ya. Isn't that right, Cable?" She looked up at me. "He wanted me...a lot...when I was pretty and had the right smell and sang the right songs—and then, Joseph, he killed me."

"Well, I'll be leaving now...good night." I said. While June was blithering I saw something on the table I didn't want to. A small bag of dope lay partially hidden under Joseph's coat sleeve. Ah...Damn! I knew she had gone back to that hard stuff and I realized that the young singer I knew just a few years ago had become a full-fledged junkie. And no doubt I was partly to blame. We were on some pretty wild trips with that stuff I picked up in Kathmandu. Eventually it would kill her. Just two years later it did.

I walked up the stairs into the sounds of the city and the night air. Sometimes it wasn't all bad. Tonight the gods of the sea sent in a high ceiling of fog and I heard seagulls fighting over a paper sack across the street. A siren wailed through the night and I could still hear Charlie Granelli's sax cryin' out *The Very Thought of You*. I reached into a pocket and took out my car keys. I was still thinking about June. Nobody can know what another person feels or how heartbreak twists and chews you in two and spits out the pieces.

173

Decisions in the Eleventh Hour

Who could I talk to about the *Klix*-strip? Who could I trust? It was late and the music from the *Blue Gardenia* was still humming in my ears. I drove back to the Winston place in Glendale. I found Boots and Fred playing strip poker with Eleanor laughing from a chair across the room. She got up to greet me and we kissed like we were college kids discovering sex on a long weekend.

Boots glanced over at us. "You two oughta get a license for that stuff. Hell, I'd have arrested you in the parking lot during my vice patrol days."

"Yes, it makes us think *you two* should be playing the strip poker," Fred chuckled. We all laughed. The more I got to know Fred, the more I liked her. Maybe she wasn't quite the dizzy dame I pegged her for in the beginning. Or maybe that's *why* I liked her, I smiled. *Maybe* she was just love hungry and made bad choices. We've all been there.

"I think the four of us gotta talk. The Feds got Krieger this morning. No telling how long it'll be before he's out. I went to visit the Austrian employee of the German Embassy who owned Krieger's Lincoln. She was all right. She told me Krieger's real last name was *Zimmer-Kleiber* and he was possibly being bankrolled by a group that called itself the *Lichter Grabstätte*."

"The Lighted Tomb," Boots said and surprised us all. "I understand some Kraut because my mother was German and spoke it with my grandmother all the time when I was a kid."

"What a peculiar name," Eleanor said. "Are they here or in Germany...or some other country?"

"Try 'em all" Boots answered. "They probably operate outta the whole damn world. I've heard of them secret organizations and such—don't trust 'em no how, no where, under no circumstances. Best not ta mess with 'em."

"So was this lady very helpful to you, then?" Eleanor asked. It was the first time I detected a hint of female jealousy...or whatever women call it. It was as if Eleanor had picked up a scent off my body or something.

"Oh, yeah," I laughed, thinking of the crazy dame. "Maya Stoldthedder is like a larger version of Marlene Dietrich. But she was charming and even offered me a warm beer."

"Ugh!" Boots exclaimed as he threw his card hand on the table. "I ain't takin' my pants off, Fredericka...and that's all there is to it!"

Fred giggled. "Well you know, Boots, it's either a penalty—or you lose."

"I'm throwin' in the towel, girl. Besides, as I tol' ya earlier, I like playin' for nickels better. To Hell with this strip crap."

We all convened in the living room. Everybody refreshed themselves and I lit up, took a deep drag, blew a smoke ring and started to talk. "So do we know anyone that we can trust who can talk to us about the strip? I get this feelin' I'm sittin' on a hot rock and it's burnin' a hole in my backside."

"Get out of it. Leave it," Boots grumbled. "It stinks, Cable. Why put your life on the line...again...for what? Them espionage folks are deadly. Everyone's expendable. Naw, I say, take your lady and run as fast as you can. Leave town..."

"Ah but he's still in possession of the strip, Boots," Eleanor interrupted. "Who's he going to hand it off to? We don't even know what we've got. Who *should* have it?

Boots kept protecting me. "If ya gotta, why don't ya dump the damn thing back in the hands of the bein's or creatures who made it? Didn't you say this...uh...this alien kid—?"

"—that's Onex Four—the one who's four hundred years young and lives in a greenhouse..."

"Yeah, that guy. Didn't ya say he wanted it?"

I knew I was grabbing at straws. But it made sense that returning the strip to the kid alien would be best...if he could make it work. But he had said he needed the other *Klix*-strip, the one Zelbacher had. If we could convince Carlton to give it up and be done with the whole mess, then maybe we'd all get home in time to see a good ball game or visit Playland at the Beach. "What do you girls think?"

Eleanor looked at me as if I were giving up our lives together. "I'm with Boots' first idea. Cable, you don't have to work. You've got me, darling. Drop it in the ocean somewhere, destroy it, burn it up in a furnace, blow it up...anything."

"I think we should return it to Onex Four. Maybe Lareet can help us," Fred responded. "I know a secret entrance to Trancas House." Now she was thinking like a detective. "If we can get in undetected, then we can try to talk Carlton out of the other strip. Then, we'll take both of them back to Onex Four's weather controlled quarters. I know the codes. I've watched people tap in the numbers on the locked chamber doors."

Eleanor was alarmed. "Cable! Fred! It's like committing suicide! Why would you want to jump right into the middle of it?" Then she turned to me. "Don't you know, Cable, Krieger's people are out to get you sooner or later?"

I got up and went over and patted Eleanor's hand. "Sorry, babe, but I don't figure it that way. I'm leaning toward Fred's point of view. Yeah, Fred, you're beginning to think like a private dick."

"I already had one of those...didn't last," she joked.

"So ya go in. Then how do ya git out of that trap with all those kraut goons hangin' around at every turn?" Boots asked.

I looked at Eleanor. I knew her heart was pounding with fear and breaking at the same time. I knew she knew that if I went back into that alien hellhole I might never come out again. But there's something peculiar about my type of gumshoe. There's a kinda silent code of ethics that won't leave him alone until the case is resolved. It wasn't possible for him to leave with all the strings undone, like leaving in the middle of an exciting movie. He had to stick around for the thrilling climax and see it through to the end. I turned to Fred.

"If you know another way into Trancas House, I'm game. But I'm goin' it alone and you gotta stay put. I already risked my skin to get you out once. I have other things I gotta concentrate on this time."

But Fred was adamant. "Well, I guess you'll just have to find the secret way by yourself, then and be done with it."

"Fred!" Eleanor cried. "What are you doing?"

Fred pointed at me. "I'm like him, Eleanor. I can't stand to see injustice done to others. And what about Carlton? Don't you even care that he's injecting himself to death?"

"Of course I care. But there's nothing I can do about it. Nor can you."

I took a shot of gin. "It may not be as bad as all that, folks. There's a good possibility that most of the people in those labyrinths don't know about Fred's secondary entrance."

"Don't bet on it, Cable," Boots warned. I remember the time we found a secret entrance to a cave filled with stolen loot. What I didn't know was that just inside two bank robbers fully armed would start firin' their pistols in the dark. They killed two of my men before the posse could do 'em in."

Eleanor had the terrible frightened look on her face that a woman gets when her world is about to implode.

"Cable, may I speak to you privately?" Eleanor asked.

We excused ourselves and she took me into her bedroom. It was a light-blue posh affair with lemon yellow curtains made of shiny silk. The bed could've slept five and her walk-in closet could double for a dining room. "Cable," she began. "I don't presume to tell you what to do. But remember what I said about what place do I truly have in your life? You're still thinking like a carefree bachelor private eye, taking the same risks you've always taken. But now there's me. Do I count, Cable? Or am I just that sometime woman you're used to...the one you can take on or off the shelf whenever you want her?"

They were good questions. To a normally sane man, what she said would've made perfect sense. I also knew this was that delicate place in a new romance where one of us could easily throw in the towel and say the party's over. But damn it all, I loved this woman and I couldn't leave her out of my life any more than I could leave my breath. I held her in my arms and rocked her with me for a minute. "I know, babe. You love a crazy guy and I don't know what to do about it." I kissed her.

"Remember what I said about *truth* to you that day when we first met? When I told you the one thing I had to have around me was truth? Well, this whole thing with your husband stinks. And it's like a canker sore festering with lies and deceit. I won't let it exist anymore. I've gotta see it through to its end, Eleanor."

She walked away a few paces. Her voice was calm and she was looking out at the night through those yellow curtains. "Funny. The thing that scares me, is caused by one of the very reasons I love you. Truth. So many men are deceitful. Not you, my darling. Oh, I don't mean other women because I know you've got a lot of momentum and it will take you a while to slow down. Yet the very thing I love in you so much is the one thing that takes you from me."

"But only until this thing is over, done, resolved, kaput."

"And if it isn't? Will I always risk being your widow before I'm your wife?"

I walked over to her. I took her into my arms and kissed her, pressing her gorgeous body into mine, feeling all those marvelous bumps and curves I so adored. "I'm the cat with nine lives, Eleanor. I can sense when

179

my time's up. And it ain't now, or tomorrow. Look...I promise as soon as Fred and I—"

"—and my sister, too. You'd do that? Take her from me again?"

"Eleanor, life's not a safe place...we don't own anybody!" I pressed. "People have to do what they have to do! Fred's a grown woman. So she doesn't make the best choices in men, but she's good and intelligent and capable. And she knows Trancas House."

Now Eleanor was crying. "I know, you think I'm weak. That I'm a cry-baby. But I've never cried so much as when I'm around you. It's so hard, Cable. I die every time you go out the door that could be leading you to some unknown possible peril."

Conversations like this could last for hours. And I didn't have hours. "I've got to go, Eleanor. All I can do is hope you understand that I gotta be me, the torn up guy you say you love, who lives on the edge because it's the only way he knows how. I told you at the beginning that I had crashed alongside the road long ago, and the best I could give you are a few pieces."

She came closer and looked up at me with those blue-green eyes, which ran now with mascara tears. She was reflective, searching out a place deep inside of her. "Funny. Things happen so fast. Yesterday, I was totally in love with you. I had never loved or given myself, as I told you, to anyone like I've given myself to you. When that happens to a woman like me, I think something deep down becomes completely committed to the one she loves. That's me. But it also comes with a woman's nature. And you may think of it as weak, but it's because I must hold back asserting myself because my heart and emotions are part of what make me desire you so and I can't take that back." Then some stronger place in her took over and she steeled herself. "So...go, my darling— and if I'm lucky enough to see you again, I'll have whatever days and nights we can have together"

"I want to marry you, Eleanor. Never in a million years could I imagine I'd be saying this to a woman at this stage of my life and the caution lights are flashing. But my heart over-rules. There. I said it. That's my truth, beautiful woman. But we gotta get through this thing first. It's kinda like the hero's quest, the journey through Hades. And when you come out at the other end, the gorgeous babe's waiting for ya."

Eleanor looked down. "If you come out. Oh, Cable!"

She flew into my arms and I kissed her with everything I had left in me. We never know when 'good-bye' becomes that final requiem at the end of a bullet.

We finally rejoined Boots and Fred. It was agreed that Fred and I would take the strip and get it back into Trancas House. Once there, we would somehow secure the other strip from Carlton Zelbacher and then proceed to give it to Onex Four with the hope that it would somehow allow him to return to his own people.

But Boots took it badly. "Ya crazy son-of-a-bitch. I thought I'd taught ya better n' that. It's suicide. For both of ya! Don't come crawlin' back to me after you're dead!"

"We promise, Boots," I said, giving the old lug an embrace. Fred hugged the old former sheriff. She had grown very fond of him.

I turned to Eleanor who steadied herself as I approached. "It'd always be like this anyway, babe. Every time I'd step out onto the street...you'd never know. I wouldn't expect you to live like that."

She tiptoed up and whispered into my ear. "I would live like that, in that fear, on that edge, hoping that you'd be with me, even for one more hour, one more day. I'll wait, darling, because I've never loved like this before and never will." She kissed me hard upon the mouth....a kiss to remember....

"By the way, thanks for the note you dropped off at the office. I never read anything like it. Somehow your words got etched inside me, just like you are..." I embraced her and kissed her once more.

"Where are we gonna stay while you're out adventurin' yourself to death, Cable?" Boots asked.

"You two stay here for a day. Then go back to your place. As long as Krieger is in custody and his goons are looking for me, I think you'll be okay. They won't suspect in a million years that we're gonna be jumpin' right in on top of 'em."

I turned and Fred and I walked out of the house. Eleanor and Boots followed us to the door. I don't know why, but it seemed strange waving good-bye to those two while Fred and I sat in my coupe together. Life twists every minute ya give it a chance to. Nothing stays the same.

The Terrors of Trancas House

Fred and I rode along for a while in silence. A cold, sticky feeling was coming over me, like some horrible, invisible thing was riding in the back seat with us. I even looked into my rear-view mirror, but nothing was there. Like one of those presences that you just seem to feel and then it starts sucking out your confidence.

Finally I had to strike up some conversation. "So why are *you* doing this, Fred?" I asked, lighting up and tossing the match into my ashtray.

"Why are *you* doing it?" she countered.

"Me? Ha! Because I'm stupid. Because I'm made that way and because I'm glued to some innate morality that good can still win. Whatever made us that way, Fred, we are what we are. You think it was easy leaving Eleanor back there?"

Fred was looking through the windshield. "No. I know it wasn't…she's totally in love, Cable. Do you *really* know that?"

I fidgeted in my seat. "I don't know what I know anymore. Just like I don't know what I feel. I'm like an animal with a one-track mind. Until this thing is finished, I can't see ahead to the next bend in the road. It comes as it comes. When we were at Vine Street I would have tossed everything aside just to have your sister beside me, breathing in her love just like a lovesick puppy."

"What happened?"

"Well, I got a dose of reality, kid. I've been a cop or P.I. for twenty years. The mold is set. I can't rip it outta me…what I am and what I've been all these years working in the streets of an ailing metropolis called L.A."

"Is there no happy medium? In England they say, 'Cheer up, because after the first sherry goes down, everything is 'tickety boo!'" She laughed.

"Well, I'm still hoping. If your sister could put up with a guy who smokes and drinks too much, still takes a second look at pretty dames, goes to Friday night fights, has no regular hours and at least once a year lays a two to one bet that someone might kill him when he starts down that next alley some night."

"I believe love can always find a way, Cable."

"I don't even know what love is, Fred. I use the word and even say it now and then when some part of me lights up inside and warm and toasty things happen, but I don't know what I experienced with Eleanor. It just felt so damned good. Which reminds me, I always wanted to ask. How did you end up with that slight British accent and your sister didn't?"

"Oh, I'm the broad that studied abroad. I went to the *very* prestigious Cheltenham Ladies' College. Even when I was a little girl, I loved the English, especially handsome and elegantly dressed English men. Our mother was Swedish-Danish, and our dad was English and Welsh. Eleanor preferred the more rugged western man, but had a very bad affair with a cowboy singer in her early twenties. So she went the other way, you know—"

"—you mean with someone like Carlton Zelbacher."

"Yep. Profoundly! Carlton impressed her mind and his imaginative, scientific brain drew her to him."

"Was she ever in love with him?" I asked, doing that strange thing the male ego does when it can't do anything about past rivals but wants to know anyway.

"No. She married him to take care of him. She has a lot more of our mother in her than I do. I knew she was unhappy as a woman in that marriage, but she's not the type to have an affair on the side."

"And you? Seems to me Berguson didn't exactly fit your elegant English gentleman image."

She drew quiet for a minute. "Hold tight, Cable...*I* was the one in love with Carlton. He was like the carefree boy who never knew the rules and played without a safety net. I was drawn to that. Berguson showed up out of nowhere, wined, dined and...well, you know. Maybe I thought I was on some sort of unfulfilled rebound..."

That floored me. Goes to show—ya never know a dame's brain.

"I thought you said you didn't have much of a nurturing nature?"

"Except when it came to Carlton. Please, Cable, this is between us. Eleanor never knew. And now it doesn't matter."

I patted her on the knee. "Well, you can trust me, kid. Do you think you can talk him out of the other *Klix*-strip?"

"I don't know. Depends on whether he still needs it for his experiments."

"So...uh...you haven't answered me. Why are you *doing* this insane thing? And don't tell me it's for Carlton."

"I told Boots and Eleanor it was because I knew another way into Trancas House...and I wanted to help out poor, sick Onex Four to get back home. But that was only partly true. I *do* want to rescue Carlton...from himself. I wanted him to know that even now I love him. That's why when Leon Berguson kidnapped me and brought me to Trancas House it was relatively easy. I saw Carlton every day and helped him."

"Did you know he was injecting himself with that al-ien...whatever you call it? And how are you going to compete with the comely Mrs. Pajabbi who is obviously in love with your mad scientist as well?"

She winced, thinking for a minute. "She can't see to his needs as I can. I can afford to get him to a rehab fa-cility and pump that poison out of his system. It's called TCG, Trans-source DNA Splicing. Kind of what you'd do with the cross-pollination of a tree, splice the different seedlings together. That's recent. Out of nowhere comes Sereba who attends Carlton at Krieger's orders, fazing me out of the picture. I got depressed, starting drinking, took a few drugs to keep me numbed up."

"But why the Pajabbi woman?"

"She's a trained nurse-technician. But because he's so damned irresistible, she proceeds to fall in love with Carlton herself! So now I can bump her out of the way and we can take Carlton back with us."

"Don't be so sure," I cautioned Fred. "We don't even know if *we'll* emerge alive from this cockeyed mess. By the way, there's something I never quite understood about the second *Klix*-strip, the one I found in the light-well over at the house. How did it really get there?"

"Carlton told me that when the flying saucer, or whatever it was, crashed in Missouri, Krieger and his goons were there on the spot even before the American emergency crews arrived."

"But how in the hell could the krauts know about it before the American military surveillance people?"

"No one knows. Maybe they have sophisticated tracking machinery or something. Who knows?"

"Go on." I urged.

"They found the *Klix*-strips at the heart of a circular drive mechanism. Rightly assuming they controlled the ship, the men removed one. But as the firemen and police arrived, Krieger ordered his men out of the craft. But sly little traitor he is, he dashed back to retrieve the second strip for himself."

A light went on. "Ah, so now Krieger has the second strip but doesn't know what to do with it. Especially since he wants to pass it over to Der Fürher's Third Reich for personal gain."

"Yes. So, he has heard of Carlton's brilliant work in a new field, 'molecular electrolitics.' He privately hires Carlton, and for a while it works until—"

"—until Carlton gets wind it's for the bad guys, both krauts and Krieger in this case—"

"—so Krieger kidnaps Carlton out of desperation—"

"—and Carlton, sensing the danger, hides the second *Klix*-strip in your light-well before Krieger's thugs can grab him."

"Well done, Cable. But Carlton doesn't tell me. In the meantime, Krieger assumes I do know and hires the dashing Leon Berguson to sweep me off my feet, trying to discover the whereabouts of the second strip—"

"—yeah, but Berguson is also a crook with ulterior motives and sensing your attachment to Carlton, not to mention Eleanor's plight in all this, extorts money from you to free Carlton and double crosses Krieger."

"Yes, but I didn't know. I thought I was in love, and Eleanor and I would do anything to get Carlton back. Now Carlton is forced to work on the originally stolen *Klix*-strip in the underground laboratory at Trancas House. Upon meeting Onex Four, he becomes obsessed.

187

He wants to help the little fellow and find out every-thing there is to know about the strip—"

"—but Onex Four informs Krieger that both strips are needed to accomplish anything worthwhile. They're not identical, but they've gotta work in tandem."

"Exactly." She affirms

"So once Krieger deduces you don't know where the second strip is—and that I have it—he shifts his efforts to hunt me down and steal it for himself and maybe, just maybe for Hitler's grand cause. In the process, he leaves a trail of blood...first Zorrie Robles, then Berguson for double crossing him."

"And God knows who else. By the way, Cable, just out of curiosity where did you hide the *Klix*-strip."

I laughed teasingly. "You got your feet on it, kid, under the mat."

We both had a hearty laugh.

We pulled off Highway One and proceeded toward Trancas House. Before we got to the turn off, Fred directed me to the right, up a very steep, very narrow red rocked road. About three-quarters of the way up, we went left and then down into a small driveway where there sat an old barn. It looked like it came out of the early 1900's. It even had the faded remnants of some lettering on the roof, an advertisement, something like *'Chew Mail Pouch Tobacco'*. We parked at the side of the barn. I reached down to the mat under Fred's feet and got the strip. I took a deep breath. If it only knew how much trouble it had caused already!

Fred led us to what looked like an old pump house, the kind that had frayed, black electrical wiring going to it. We entered into a small, dark room. She took my hand and squeezed it, like a campfire girl on an exciting excursion. "This is it?" I asked.

"Lareet found it when he was playing here one day. There's a small stairway or ladder going down to a tunnel that leads to the laboratories. They must have dug it for an emergency exit."

"Yeah. Good ol' Krieger. I hope he stays with the Feds for a few lifetimes. But I know it won't happen. The German Embassy will get him out."

"Just the thought of it gives me the chills."

"If you know what's good for you, you'll turn around and go now, Fred, and don't look back...and don't worry about me."

Her face showed surprise. "You know I can't do that. I've explained all my reasons. I got you into this, Cable. It's only fair that I help get you out."

"This is no time to be a heroine, Fred. You're young... ya got a life ahead of you. You know what's down there as well as I do."

"Too bad, it's the two of us, Cable Denning. Besides, I can't let Carlton die without..."

"Alright! You're starting to sound like a broken record. But don't ever say I didn't try to talk you out of this insanity."

I helped Fred move two large sheets of rusting corrugated metal. Underneath there was a circular hole, maybe three-feet in diameter sealed with piece of wood that looked like the top to a large wine barrel. We had forgotten a flashlight, but Fred said there was a railing on one side of the descending ladder.

We quietly fumbled our way down the secret ladder. At the bottom, a narrow passage wound through the bowels of the lower chambers of Trancas House. Finally we came out into a corridor. Everything appeared to be amazingly quiet. Fred knew the way to Zelbacher's lab and she quickly led us through halls and passages. The main laboratory area where Krieger and I had originally arrived via the elevator-closet was deserted. Everything was piled high in boxes as if someone had given orders to pack up when Krieger had been arrested.

Finally we arrived at Carlton Zelbacher's door. Sitting down in front of it with her back propped up against the wall sat Sereba Pajabbi. Up further and fast asleep on the floor lay the boy Lareet. That sad look she still wore upon her face told a lot of stories.

She started to get up. "Shh..." I whispered. "We don't wanna wake up the goons. Is Zelbacher in?"

Sereba looked at Fred. She knew the score. "Everyone is gone. Dr. Zelbacher is still here with Onex Four. I know not of any others. Lareet and I were left to attend..."

"We need to see the doc. Now," I urged her.

Fred reached into her pocket and withdrew a key. "It's okay, Sereba."

Just then Lareet woke up and rubbed the sleep out of his eyes. "Oh, Miss Fredericka...and Mr. Denning. Very pleased to see you again. Even though I am worried about Dr. Zelbacher."

"Good to see ya, kid. Whatta ya mean?"

"He is changing. Very fast."

Sereba started to cry. "I told him no more injections. Too much too soon...you know what will happen!" she sobbed.

Fred was upset as well as she unlocked the door to Carlton's quarters. Once inside it looked like a hurricane had blown through his lab. "Carlton! Carlton? It's Fred. Are you here?"

"Too many voices! Don't come in!" Zelbacher shouted from another part of the apartment. "Go home, Fredericka. Did you bring Sereba? I need Sereba to inject me."

"I'm here, too, doc," I said with a little authority. "I've got the other strip and I need to talk to you."

There was a long silence. Then his voice changed to a higher pitch and kept dropping in and out like a weak radio signal. "Turn off all the lights. I'll come to you."

We did so and the four of us waited in the middle of Zelbacher's cluttered laboratory. Soon a figure appeared in the shadows. But even in the semi-dark we could see the body had been altered—the entire outline of his human form glowed with a green luminosity! "Damn! What in the hell happened?" I asked firmly.

He was breathing hard. "I should have listened to you, Sereba. Now the cells are so rapidly changing that I am in a constant state of pain and nausea." The handsome little Indian woman ran over to Carlton to hug him. He backed away. "No! Please, Sereba! You'll be radiated with the poison which I am becoming." One could tell Fred's heart was breaking as she felt the imminent separation between her and Carlton. Plus he had called upon Sereba and not her to assist him. Yeah, she had lost him.

"Tell you what, Zelbacher. I don't think you've got a lot of time left. As I said, I've got the other strip. Before Krieger gets out of the slammer and his goons resume

191

hunting us all down for keeps, I want you to give me the other strip and we'll give them both to Onex Four. You knew that both strips would allow the poor suffering alien to go home. Yet you delayed, why?

There was just enough light in the room to reveal his face somewhat. He looked at Fred like a forlorn cat. "I'm sorry Fred. I made such a mess of everything. How's Eleanor?"

"She's in love with Denning," she answered.

I raised an eyebrow and did a double–take at Fred. Zelbacher glanced over to me. "That's good. She always liked the adventuresome type. I remember the cowboy she told me about. "

"Excuse me, Zelbacher, this is not the family hour. Now, are you gonna hand over the other strip or do I have to take it by conkin' you on the noggin?"

"Cable! Take it easy, he's in pain," Fred admonished me.

"Oh yes, Onex Four can help you, Doctor Zelbacher," Lareet spoke up in that wise little voice of his.

I could see Zelbacher's face a little clearer now. The left side of his face had turned a rather shiny, sick gray. His arms fit differently in their sockets and his clothes hung on him like the incredible shrinking man. Now his voice had a resignation to it. "Yes...I'm ready. I should have done it all along. But Krieger wanted little gold stars from Hitler and to profit by keeping both strips and selling them to the highest bidder. If Germany had the power of the *Klix*-strips, Hitler would rule the planet hands down, no question. That's why I hid the one strip you found, Mr. Denning. My estates were becoming de- pleted from the monies I had privately invested in developing much of what you see here. The rest of it was furnished by Krieger's *Lichter Grabstätte*. They also have a vested interest in things and if our little junior alien should obtain both strips and levitate home, then everyone in this room is dead by their orders."

"So what else is new?" I said, my voice tinged with sarcasm. "So you woulda sold out that little guy down the hall breathin' for his life...as long as there was time for you and Krieger to make a little profit."

"I hate Krieger. He betrayed everyone. I just wished to replenish the funds I had depleted." Just then Carlton collapsed. We put some lights on and covered him with a blanket. He was shivering. He spoke haltingly "In...in my pocket, Denning. Take it. It connects to the other strip electrically, but you must...must put the right ends together. There's a wheel chair down the hall...Sereba, get it and take me to Onex Four. Now...before it's too late!" He looked terrible. His skin, mouth and ears were developing a whitish-green color, while his eyes were turning to slits and the pigment in his eyes were turning into a deep black.

Rochelez and Intelligent Design

Lareet led us down the twisted halls and corridors until I could feel that strange warm damp like a Swedish sauna and that green glow seemed to emanate out of the walls. Lareet smiled as he quickly punched in the combination to the outer door to Onex Four's lair. We entered, each of us in our own world of silence. As we wheeled Carlton Zelbacher in, I could tell immediately that the stifling air in Onex Four's chamber was having a bad effect on the poor little creature.

A kind of green glowing steam was rising around little Onex Four's body as Lareet approached within a few feet. The strange one motioned for Lareet to turn on the translator. He was leaning against what appeared to be the same low metal cart where I had first observed him days ago. "I have brought the ones to save you, Kylell," the boy said with a kind of happy pride to be helping his friend.

"Kylell?" I asked.

The slow-moving alien looked us over. He glanced at me, but addressed the others. *"Welcome, and thank you. Miss Winston, Sereba. Dr. Zelbacher I am sorry you are ill. I told you that your physical body could not sustain the vibration. Please know I cannot help you. The time is over for your mortal pod."* Fred and Sereba gasped and each held on to an arm of Zelbacher's. Then he looked at me. *"May I call you Denning? Please call me Kylell. That is my real name. Onex Four is the name Krieger gave me before we could communicate."*

"I don't think we've got a lotta time, Kylell," I said. "Tell us what to do. I see your assistants have deserted you."

"All is good now. I have instructed Lareet." The little alien summoned Lareet forward. With his palms extended, he must have somehow communicated with Lareet's mind, for at once the boy began to press buttons and prepare things.

"We gotta get on with it Kylell." I urged.

Then Lareet approached me. Without a word I handed him my strip. Then the boy went to Zelbacher.

The shivering man reached into his coat pocket and handed Lareet the second strip. The boy bowed his head toward the doctor and went back to Kylell. The latter mentally instructed the boy and Lareet took both strips and stuck them into two slots on what appeared to be a large crystal orb, not unlike the kind Zorrie Robles had used, only twenty times larger. There was a wonderful hum...loud, but oddly, didn't hurt your ears but kinda lulled you. I noted, also, the young alien's voice had been modified since the last time I met him as if he had to push up the energy for it to work.

I stepped forward. Fred, Sereba and Zelbacher remained a few feet behind me. "What's next? I've got this terrible feeling...Krieger and his goons are gonna want revenge...and soon."

Kylell remained calm, looking directly at me with those black eyes. *"We will dispense with time for the moment, Denning. Because you have stepped beyond concern for your own existence, and given me the gift of returning home to be with my own, I in turn bestow a gift to you. I meld my being with yours so you may experience Rochelez...the experience of allness. You already have a finely sensitized intuition. This shall be enhanced by your vision of Rochelez."*

Suddenly I felt myself being pulled apart and then together again. The entire room disappeared. I found myself in every corner of the universe and nowhere in the same instant. It was like a glorious drunk without the hangover or unhappy ending, or waking up with a babe who doesn't look so hot as she did the night before. Everything was one. I didn't have to worry about me anymore because I *wasn't* anymore. We, I, were

195

synonymous. Yet I was aware of being this precious point of something wonderful, a kind of individual identity, at once everywhere. I was *always* me, always everyone, always everything. The bliss that resulted from this sensation skyrocketed me out of my human awareness so that I could no longer see the long-suffering gray lines of nothingness that had become my life, an angry, clawing-at-the-wall nobody who scrounged in the garbage can of a wounded society of beings. Suddenly consciousness was *freedom* from concern of perpetuating a physical body any more.

Everywhere, the sky was filled with colors unimaginable as I was pulled across countless, endless heavens of stars. But in-between the astounding stellar nebulae that turned the cosmos into shapes, sizes and colors too staggering to comprehend, something else inside of me spun and reeled like a kaleidoscope of color and knowing! What our eyes may mistake as vast, empty spaces, the canvas of eternity sparkled *within* it, filled with warmth and love and laughter, though I saw no one. Yet, somehow, I knew their mirth, the vitality, never-ending youthfulness, and I knew why. It was because there never was an answer to creation, because there never was a *question*. Only humans asked *why*, in their ignorant, remnant state of being as neither gods nor animals. Animals never ask why. And *Rochelez* was coming home to some state of being I never left.

I came out of it feeling pretty good. My chest felt clear and my heart had calmed. I was sure Kylell was giving me the equivalent of a smile. "Zowse! Where am I? It felt kinda like the trip dope'll take you on, except this was the real thing! I'd like to spread that feeling around a bit."

"Altered states. The chemistry of the mind is an opiate, Denning. I am happy for you that you chose to take the experience openly. What you have done is glimpsed the very first layer of cosmic truth. I know what truth means to you, I have felt it since the first day we communicated."

"I realize time is of the essence here—but may I ask one more question?"

"I know your question, Denning. What is life? Is there an intelligent design? Everything in the universe is chemistry. In your language you may say all things are little electric arcs of energy, fueled by chemistry. Balanced energy, balanced mind and body. Even your essence self, what you call spirit or soul, is a combinative form of chemistry. The difference being, <u>this</u> is the core place of consciousness, and as such, is the perfect coming together of all the elements in creation. If you ask of intelligent design, you are asking "did you create yourself? But it is difficult to understand how chemistry creates orderly 'blueprints', I think you call them. When these combine electrically, they are neither chemical nor elemental, but fundamental. Thus the body is created to express and manifest spirit. That is why we study you. Humans are blessed with the whole compliment of the elements to manifest spirit through the physical body. But beware. Other species of beings harness the essence energy you call <u>soul</u>. They do not interfere with your populations because they grow you as a crop so they may feed off of your personal energy as your bodies decease. They are

vampires of a kind, you would say. But beware. You can prevent usurpation only by preventative thought. "

I was floored at what this young being was telling me. "It sounds insane, Kylell, and it's more than I can comprehend. I get the chemistry thing...but you go beyond—"

"*—be gentle with yourself, Denning. Do not attempt to comprehend what you cannot yet accept.*"

"Thank you, Kylell." I didn't understand much, but got the message that chemistry is what we are and deal with, every day in this fucked up existence humans calling 'living.'

"*Now that you have experienced Rochelez, new insights will come.*"

"What was even stranger about that trip, Kylell, was that I felt comfortable. It was like a homecoming that I didn't know I'd missed until you showed me..." I looked over at the others. Except for Carlton who seemed to be fading, the others were looking straight ahead to Kylell and the magic of these moments.

"*That is because you are not native to this land. Things have been Terra-formed to suit you, but this is not your natal planet. Why is it you look so often to the stars on a quiet night and dream of home? We are always space travelers, returning to our points of origin.*"

Shivers went down my spine. I have heard the reference to 'home' being not on this Earth...but Kylell had hit a homer just at this moment and it made me think again. I *was* always restless, unsettled, never feeling native here on this globe. Yet it had its beauty. Maybe somewhere in me, it was the psychological escape from the relentless grind of the city, which calls out for your blood and death daily, devours you and then spits you out until you're pushing up daisies at Forest Lawn. "Thank you. I don't respect many humans...in fact, damn it, I like you...and your truth...and you're not even human!"

Then he took a deep breath. I knew he was suffering and needed to get on with the process now. *"I like you, too, Denning. You call these beings that like each other friends? We have such chosen companions where I come from."*

"Yeah, Kylell, *friends*. Here they're kinda rare. But you'd better start pushin' those buttons. I can feel you're getting weaker. Use the strips now, my alien friend. Leave no trace of them for the krauts."

"One thing more, Denning. Your species feels divided, discontent, uprooted because it has been manipulated many times over for many thousands of your years to please the needs of others. These beings used your kind for their own purposes. That is the reason for the unsettled feeling you experience. One day my kind and others like it will work on turning your original genus back to the complete complement of the genetic matrix code. This was your birthright. I am sorry it was altered." The little creature waved his free hand slowly at me.

"Do you have love where you come from?" I blurted out, because that was what I was feeling in this moment.

"Ayrr. It is the fabric consciousness of all universes. Thank you, Denning, I will remember you. And who knows, one night we may meet in our dream time. Farewell. "

Kylell signaled Lareet to press the orange and blue buttons as he tilted his head and waved good-bye to the

199

others. There was a mighty increase in the hum and a beautiful bright yellow light filled the room, and an aura, like a big light-green bubble surrounded my little alien friend. Then, still hanging on to the mobile cart, he disappeared right before our eyes.

I felt elated. I was also trying to digest some of what he had said in those last sentences. I wish I could've written 'em down. I knew they'd probably be forgotten next week. What is it that finally sticks with us? Maybe *Ayrr*. Something about us being screwed over by the hidden, oppressive powers, who somehow toned down our full potential, which was housed in...what was it he said? Ah, the genetic matrix code. I looked over at Fred. She was crying. Carlton had died while I was taking my trip. Both she and Sereba were grieving over someone I never really knew, a good lookin' guy with silver temples and a nice haircut now slumped over in his chair. But he was no longer handsome. In fact, he had become downright monstrous looking—his mouth hung open, the eye-slits watering a green substance. Oh...well, I guess if he got no other rewards in this world, just returning the strip and sacrificing his life for the betterment of all creatures must count for something.

Chapter 9

DEATH BECOMES YOU

Fred and I ran up the stairs to the pump house. Sereba and Lareet had stayed behind to attend Carlton Zelbacher's body and await the cops. We raced back to L.A. because I had the sinking feeling players had shifted on the chessboard back home. I had to make sure that Eleanor and Boots were okay. They were anxiously awaiting us when we drove up. I told them they have to change locations and go back to Vine Street. I just had a hunch. I kissed Eleanor but she held on to me. Her eyes were misting.

"Oh, Lord Cable. You can't know the anguish I felt while you were gone. I thought of every possible horrible thing...I even thought you and Fred might have—"

"—Not yet, Doll. I'll tell ya when my number's up. Now, do as I say....please! I gotta get back to my office for a while....some loose ends to tie up."

I started out the door and Eleanor followed me. "You're reverting, Cable. I can feel it."

"Reverting?"

"Back to your old self. What happened to the vulnerable and beautiful lover who intoxicated me in Santa Barbara or on Vine Street...and couldn't let me go?"

"He's still there, kid. I told you. Until something is finished, I'm a one-trick pony heading for the finish line. Besides, the fat lady ain't singin' yet, is she?"

She turned to go. "I don't know. She could sing any minute. Then I could lose you forever. I could never bear that, my love. I think I'm biting my nails for the first time in my life. Please come back to me tonight."

"I'll take you to get a manicure, part of that package deal for a honeymoon in Sierra Valley."

She lit up as only a woman can light up when she's been told she's going to belong to someone. "Oh, Cable I can't wait to be with you...us alone again. Sierra Valley, you crazy man? Where's that?"

"Me neither, babe. It's a big expansive valley just north of Reno." She ran back to me and threw her arms around me. Holding me, she whispered things in my ears only the gods should hear. But I heard them. '*When I have you and I meld my whole self into you, my life is complete. And there I lie with you in the middle of paradise, feeling your lips softly upon mine, your strong hand holding my womanhood there between my legs, and your nipples pressing upon my own breasts until I can hardly breathe anymore—I am then in ecstasy, Cable, the one I want always with me...and no one else ever... until our dear fat lady sings.*'

I held her tight and kissed her. This woman had a way of moving me, coming up with the unexpected from what seemed the deepest place a woman had in her. However, I had forgotten something. "Uh, babe, I know Fred will probably take you aside and say it more diplomatically. But I think it's okay for me to tell you. Carlton died. Those damned injections just finally did him in."

Eleanor stood there as she silently slipped her arms off of my body and let them fall to her side. "I guess I knew, Cable. There's something else you don't have to tell me. I knew Fred was in love with him for years. I didn't say anything. Because I loved both of them so much."

I grabbed her by the wrist and squeezed it. "I'm sorry, Doll. Better get packed. I'll see ya tonight at the Vine Street house. Grab Boots and Fred…and go as soon as you can." Then I turned and walked to my little black coupe.

I don't know where the time went, but it was already early Wednesday evening when I parked on the street across from my office. Krieger and company had given me a case of the willies about approaching my place of business. Too many unpleasant surprises in so few days put me on guard. But it looked okay. I crossed the street and went up to my office. I entered quietly. Not a sound. I drew my .38 just in case and slipped quietly into my bedroom. There in pink panties and bra lay a reclining Ida Latney! I started to dart out of the room when she awakened.

"Oh! Mr. Denning! I'm sorry—I'm not dressed—I didn't know that you were coming here—thank God you're safe." She attempted to cover up her near naked body. "I'm embarrassed, but it was so hot up here.."

I laughed. "It's okay, Ida. I'm glad you're here. Now, while you get your clothes on, I'm gonna pour us a mighty fine drink. "Eighty-proof or Shirley Temple for you?"

She was still holding her hand over her near-naked chest. "Whew! Maybe tonight I should have some of the real stuff, don't you think, Mr. Denning? My nerves are so shaky. I was worried about you, I didn't know what to think."

"Absolutely! You deserve it, kid. Two gin tonics coming up!"

Soon Ida joined me and we toasted. "To you and your steadfast loyalty, Ida. And to me, for having completed most of...most of what? What in the hell *have* I been doing for the past few days? Well, let's just toast to success!"

Ida lifted her glass and looked at me with those longing warm eyes of hers. "To success, Mr. Denning...."

I meandered over to my desk to gander at the phone messages. "Anything important?"

"I don't know. An impatient Lieutenant Keith called. Mrs. Finian wants to know if you've caught her husband yet with his secretary. Oh, and one other call, from a very nice man named Albert Newley. But that was a social call."

"Ha! Al Newley. Yeah, I will call that old son-of-a-bitch. He was one of the best cops I ever knew. An honest one." But first I had to call Keith. I knew somehow the news would not be good. I got the number and he came on the line.

"About goddamn time! Krieger, Zimmer-Kleiber or whoever the fuck he is shot two plainclothes Feds, stole a car, killed the driver, went over to your Marlene Dietrich character's apartment, you know the one at 4600 Los Feliz, nailed her in Apt. #201 and for all we know, has rejoined the gang you keep telling me about."

It hit me like a sledgehammer on a rock pile. Only my head was the rock. I hated this son-of-a-bitch Krieger for murdering Maya Stoldthedder. I've always loved bigger-than-life characters. I shoulda gotten her out myself. Now it was too late. "Well, then, Lieutenant, seems we have unwelcome news for both of us." I then proceeded to tell him of Trancas House and the goings on there and that Sereba and Lareet Pajabbi were waiting there with Zelbacher's body. "Now, remember, as soon as you enter the house, to your left is an elevator that looks like a closet. Get in; punch *one* and down ya go. You'll have to figure out the rest by yelling for Mrs. Pajabbi and her son. The underground labs are a maze."

"Why in the hell didn't you tell me this sooner, Denning? I could have you brought in on withholding evidence."

"Because I had to make sure I wasn't dreaming it all. Yeah, and be my guest. Haul me in. Give me safe refuge behind bars for a week or two Now that Krieger's on the loose again, count my days as numbered, Lieutenant."

"You scare too easy, Denning. Naw, I won't bust you this time. But I'll get you for something someday." Keith laughed as he hung up.

Not being a drinker, Ida began to show the effects of two pretty stiff gin tonics I had prepared for her. I could tell she was upset and worried but trying to conceal it. "Oh, dear, Mr. Denning. You have been through a lot. I'm always surprised—and of course, happy…when you come back alive from all your dangerous assignments. I wish you didn't have to …"

"Ha! Yeah…like a bad penny I show up anyhow. Well, I surprise myself sometimes, like the proverbial cat, ending up on his paws."

"I…I think…you're a good penny…may I inquire as to who this Krieger character is?"

"Ya don't wanna know, kid. Believe me, Krieger would come up as one of evil's names, if there was a list.

I started counting on my fingers. "Since I've known him...only a few days, mind you...he's killed five people in cold blood."

Ida shivered like someone had walked over her grave. "Oh, dear God! How can there be such people in the world?"

"Hell, I read somewhere that it's pretty much how nature balances itself, Ida. Some to give life, some to protect it, some to take it. I dunno, with humans, it's probably more complicated than that.

Ida took another stiff drink. "You know how I feel, Cable....I've already embarrassed myself once in my life by telling you."

"It's safe with me, kid. And ya know, Ida. I do like you...a lot...and respect you. You see, I'm still holdin' out for you, that someday you'll meet that great young man and get off the jag of wanting to be with some guy old enough to be your Pop."

"I told you, I never even looked at the age.... it's *you*, the man inside I admire and—"

"—Uh...we'd better get on with it, Ida. Now, how desperate was Mrs. Finian? I know she's got that hot Irish temper."

Ida pouted a bit and poured herself another stiff gin and tonic. "She seemed somewhat angry. I think you'd better call her."

I got Melina Finian's number and it rang. "Hello?" a voice with a pretty thick Irish accent answered.

"Mrs. Finian. Cable Denning here. How are you?"

"No thanks to yer sorry soul I got meself in jail last night."

"In jail?! What did you do, Mrs. Finian."

"Wells, y'see, I took me rollin' pin in me purse and went down to that evil woman's desk at me husband's place o' work. There I chased 'er 'round that desk until me temper got so the much o' me that I smacked 'er in the rear, I did!"

"Oh, no, Mrs. Finian. Did you injure her badly?"

"Not a bruise, she was awearin' a corset....the hussy! But me own husband called the coppers and after chasin' that no-good of a husband o' mine around *his* room, they dragged me away like a common criminal!"

"So, you are okay now...and who bailed you out?"

"Me own husbandman! And ta think I had berated 'im so. Turned out it wasn't he who was fiddlin' with the wench, but his partner, Mr. Socal. Bernard was coverin' fer that philanderin' scoundrel."

"Oh, my. So it's all straightened out now, Mrs. Finian?"

"It is, Mr. Denning. But keep me fifty dollars. Ya earned it for *not* showin' up when you were supposed to."

"Well, thank you, Mrs. Finian. You know what they say: 'all's well that ends well', huh?"

"Sure 'tis....good-bye, Mr. Denning." She hung up and both Ida and I laughed heartily. She was looking at me...looking for something in my eyes that might invite her. I made sure she didn't find it. I fixed us both another drink. I needed to get numb and release all that heaviness that had been hanging over me the last week or two.

"I think you should call Mr. Newley. He seemed anxious... to speak with you." Ida said, this time her voice a little slurred. "I guess I'm through here. Do you want me to go home now?"

"No. Let me call Al Newley. Then I'll walk you home. The night air'll do us both good."

"Thanks. That would be nice."

I got the long-distance operator. "Yeah...I'd like to reach one Albert Newley, Lake Tahoe, California, please."

Soon the phone rang at the other end and I heard an old familiar voice. "I sure in hell hope it's you, Cable!" the voice yelled at the other end. He had the voice of a lumberjack and the handshake of a professional wrestler. He stood about six-foot and must have weighed a good two hundred muscular pounds.

"Al, you ol' son-of-a-bitch, how are ya?" I declared.

"Where'n the hell have you been? You're a tough guy to reach! So...what has one of my favorite private dicks been up to? I often think of you out there pounding your haunts in that cesspool of a city you live in. Quit it, Cable. Come up to paradise here and join an ol' drinkin' buddy by the lake."

"You know me, Al. City-bred. Someone needs to clean up the vermin crawlin' around in this city."

"Well, suit yourself. I'm inviting you, Cable, for a few days' vacation, on me. You see, old comrade in arms, I help run the famous Fire Falls at Glacier Point in Yosemite. You know, at 9:00 p.m. we send a ton of White Fir burnin' coals down a three-thousand foot drop, creating one of the most spectacular sights anywhere!"

I had heard of the Fire Falls. But I'd never been. It might work perfectly as a pre-honeymoon before I took Eleanor to Reno to get hitched. Even though she was still married and her husband was dead. I thought about that. "You know, that sounds like something I could use right now, Al. What's the scoop?

"Well, the government will be closing down the firefalls in a couple of weeks. The military is gonna be using the area, I guess as a base and they can't have a beacon like the firefalls possibly drawing the attention of enemy aircraft...that being a concern these days. So when can you come, Cable?"

"How about tomorrow? I'll have three others with me, if that's okay?"

"What...no single babe? That doesn't sound like you, Cable. Are you slipping here, or my cop sense might tell me there's more to it, knowing you...."

"Ya got it, Al. But there is a babe, too." I could see Ida's reaction and she gulped down the rest of her drink at that news.

"Well, wonderful. More than a one-night stand, then?"

"Yep. More than a one-night stand. I'm gonna probably get hitched to the dame."

There was a long pause at the other end. "Am I hearing right? The connoisseur of a hundred delicious fillets trading all that in for one dish?"

"It kinda looks that way. So, how do we coordinate?"

He filled me in on all the details. The trip fit perfectly into what I had already planned for Eleanor. I'd dash outta here tonight, get some sleep with my babe at Vine Street. Then the four of us would start out for Yosemite bright and early, get to State Route 41 outside of Fresno and stay at the Ahwahnee Hotel in the valley, just below Glacier Point. We said good-bye and I lit up another cigarette. I glanced across at Ida who was now sitting in my client's chair. There was a slight frown on her face, but more than that a kind of resignation, the kind that tells you that you just lost something that meant a lot to you. And maybe there's no hope that it would ever come back.

She looked like her friend had just deserted her and there she stood stranded in a desert of strangers with an uncertain future.

"You really love her, don't you?" Ida asked.

"Yes. I told you at the café. Remember what you said to me? That knowing it, you could work with me and not think about that day when I might need you."

She giggled a slightly tipsy laugh. "I said that? Yes, I did, didn't I? But you know, Mr. Denning, women change their minds all the time." She kicked off her shoes. "You know something? How would you like to think of me as your last fling, your bachelor party without the bachelors! I would like another drink to help you celebrate your upcoming betrothal... suddenly I'm very thirsty... if you don't mind."

"Don't you think you've had enough, Ida? You're not used to so much booze, kid..."

"How...how do you know what I do behind closed doors, Mr. Cable Denning?" she prattled. She had entered that aggressive state when you dared to say what you wouldn't when you were sober. I braced myself. "Behind...behind closed doors I do three things I've never told anyone. First, I write in my diary...uurrrp! Then I drink honeyed whiskey with hot water in a snifter...which I learned from you." Her voice lowered and she whispered almost inaudibly as she looked down at the floor. "And last of all, I fantasize about you. And when it gets too much for me, I masturbate until the edge is gone and I can cry myself to sleep." She put her glass down on the desk, got up and started to take her blouse off. She threw it on the floor and turned to face me. "What's wrong with *me*? What's wrong with these breasts, these pretty pink nipples and this soft young skin, Cable Denning? Why don't I rate with you?"

She was sobbing now and I felt helpless. Do I go to her? Do I stay back? Do I just let her run it out of her system? Ida's sudden action brought on the weirdest feeling. It was like I was at a strip show and protecting my daughter at the same time. "Ida...this isn't what should be happening right now and this isn't the right time to be discussing—"

"—Please! Let me continue, Mr. Denning." She was slurring and swaying a little bit more every minute. "I may never get this opportunity again or have the nerve to do what I'm doing now. What *is* the right time to get to you? When you're out or disappeared for three days? When you're chasing someone who could put a bullet in your back? When you're lying passed out on your bed from too much gin? When you're on the phone laughing with someone else or trying to figure out a new client's personality so you can work with them? When? When? Tell a twenty-seven year-old virgin *when*!" She sobbed. I sat quietly looking up at her. She came over and poured herself a drink of straight gin, leaving out the tonic this time. She took a long gulp and set the glass back down. "By the way, your glasses are dirty. I never get a chance to clean them properly. You have no dish soap here."

"Well, you know—an ol' died-in-the-wool bachelor's habit...I just rinse 'em with hot water. What can I say?"

She didn't answer me, instead she slipped off her skirt and let it fall to her ankles. "Now...these legs, these thighs.... What's the matter with them?" I could see the healthy mound of dark pubic hair through her pink panties. "Do you know what a woman fantasizes about? She hopes what she has to offer physically will stimulate the man she loves mentally so he may desire her. Or maybe even...love her...someday. That's what she hopes for. But do you know what most women get? They get laid. That's what they get. And after a while that gets old. That's why I don't do it. I'm old-fashioned enough to believe sex can be part of love. Is that stupid or naive? Is that what you found with your new dream woman...*love*?"

Then she just melted onto the floor, wilting down with her head in her hands, whimpering. I came over and helped her over to the sofa. I put a blanket around her legs. I spoke gently to her. "This is crazy, kid. And I'm not putting you down. I agree with most everything you say. Dames think like that, Ida. I just never heard you say it."

"I...I've got a lot more things in me than you can imagine. Things in two years you never cared enough to know about. I got a lot of things in me, a lot of good qualities. Things you'd be proud to know that dance inside me when I think about you and me..."

But, listen, Ida. I thought we agreed..."

Suddenly she threw her arms around me and bawled like a baby. "Take me! Please! Take me now...even if it never happens again...I can't live with

212

the obsession...not anymore! Let me find out you're horrible or that loving you is disgusting. Let me find it out for myself, so I won't be haunted and obsessed anymore."

Suddenly the instinctive animal in me forced my lips onto Ida's to quiet her. Swelling up from within me was that primal desire that made all men out of the same cloth, that made them know that it was this instant that nature dictated he impregnate every woman who offers herself, surrenders to his manhood. I tried to beg off her lips but she held me there with her arms holding my head against her face. "Ida! I...I don't want to do this—to hurt you or anyone."

"Ever since I've worked for you I've heard you talk about *truth*, that you're a truth man, and all that matters is *truth*. So what is your truth in this moment, Mr. Denning?"

"That I want you, kid." There, I said it. I blanked out all the moral crutches and blurted out what my primordial maleness demanded of me in that moment. "Are you sure?"

"Yes! Yes! Please." she whispered.

I took her up into my arms and carried her into the bedroom. While I took my clothes off I watched Ida Latney take off her bra and panties and lay there on the bed, her arms open, awaiting me. The powerful instinctive passions lit me up like a blowtorch and I sprang on top of her, squelching any possibility that she change her mind now. The sexual momentum came like a steam locomotive and when I felt her thick, throbbing pussy so wet for me, I became a rapist, a forceful thing out of the night, bent on the conquering of her womanhood, blinded with this thought only.

She squirmed and groaned as only a woman who has unleashed her passions can sound. "Cable...Cable...!" she sighed with a deep, wheezy voice I had never heard out of her before. "I mean it. I will never regret this moment. I want you...oh, I want you...!" I pinned her arms back and opened her legs with my hips, sidling back and forth. She was so open that I entered her with no assistance from either of our hands. If she was a virgin, then my hardness quickly penetrated the hymen because she didn't wince for an instant. But her desire was far too advanced to allow any pain to disrupt the pleasure of her orgasms. Again and again she moaned and shrieked the song of ecstasy, that little death that closes out one part of us and opens up another. I found myself driving into her, spurting my cum into her and smiling at the same time. In one moment we both cried and laughed together, as if the privilege I was taking with this young woman was equally fulfilling to her.

It must have lasted for forty-five minutes. Dripping wet from perspiration, I rolled off of her and collapsed by her side. "Whew!" I chortled, "this sure beats Friday night at the fights!"

She hit me on the shoulder. "Cable Denning...how can you? Do you have any idea of what I've just experienced with you?"

I didn't want to ruin the moment. So I shut up. Instead I stroked her hair and sucked gently on her nipples a little as a sort of affectionate nightcap. We said nothing, but simply lay there together looking up at my old plaster ceiling. A neon sign from down the street blinked on and off with a pink-blue and bounced off the far wall.

The phone was ringing. I looked at my watch. Eleanor! It was getting on to 10:30 p.m. "I've got to go, toots." I leaned up on my elbow and took a very good look at Ida's glowing face. "You know, kid, you were wonderful. Believe it or not, I will always remember this night. Uh…can you still work for me?"

She turned her head to look at me. "I…I don't know…I risked everything…maybe even not being the same…afterward…."

"Do you know I came into you…unprotected?"

"I know. I wanted it that way. I would have hated something between us, I mean, like a piece of rubber."

"And what if you get pregnant?"

"I *hope* I get pregnant. It's you…it's only you I've ever wanted. And I'll raise our child with the same beautiful love you loved me with tonight. And don't worry, I'm not the kind to get a man wrapped up in a paternity suit."

I thought the dame was nuts. How do women think? Having a baby by some older guy who may or may not be able to supply milk money! But there must be some even more ancient thing going on inside the female brain. The event of motherhood, nurturing, perpetuating her own kind. What was it? Because I noticed that once women become mothers, more often than not the guy gets tossed to the back of the line. All of a sudden he's done his siring work, she's with child…and no love is more powerful than a mother's protective, overseeing love. So, in the end, the guy is simply a breeder for nature. Maybe that's why in the wilds, males hang out together and only fuck during the breeding season. I don't know. Then it's back again to the ol' bachelor life. Well, it was true for at least some species...

We both showered together and almost ended up on the shower floor doing it again. But I pulled myself together, got dressed and came to say good-bye to the lovely young woman I had just seduced...or had she seduced *me*? Guys get confused about this, ya know.

"So what if you're not pregnant? Would you still come back to work for me? I mean, I really need ya, Ida. I've a feelin' business is gonna pick up after this stupid war."

She smiled up at me, combing her hair out. "I don't think I could ever be very far away from you, Mr. Denning..."

"Cable...from now on...around us...just the two of us...call me Cable...like you did during...uh, certain moments of sensual pleasure."

"I did?" she laughed. "Okay. Cable." She tiptoed up and kissed me deeply. "Thank you. Thank you for all the rest of my life. Do you know when you might be back?"

"Not sure. We're leaving tomorrow morning, going to Yosemite to visit ol' Al Newley. Then we're off to Reno—"

"—To marry her." She looked down. "No matter how many times I tell myself I'm not going to be jealous...I get jealous. You don't have to worry about it, though. It's something I'll deal with. But you know I wouldn't want to be someone on the side. I would hate to be the bosses' girl Friday, who fills in when there's no one else."

"I know that, Ida. I would never expect that and let me remind you, I'm also normally a true-blue kinda guy. Let's face it...Mr. Gin and you?...I didn't have a chance. I told you this was a one-time-only trip. So maybe now you might find—"

"—that handsome Prince Charming you've been telling me about? Who's going to show up in my life? Well, maybe. But how can a woman be with someone else when she's given herself to a man whom she's loved forever?"

I couldn't touch that one with a thirty-foot pole, but I smiled and drew her young body into mine. "You're the best, kid. Can you be here next Wednesday? I'll call you no later than 6:00 p.m. and let you know when we'll be back."

She put her arms around me one last time. I could feel her pussy still pulsing as she leaned into me. "I wish you happiness, Cable Denning. Truly, I do. I take responsibility for my share of everything that's happened between us. I'll wait for your call...." She walked out and it was almost like she took a little part of me out with her.

I walked to my coupe more muddled in my brain than before. What had I done? By acting on an instinct the moral standards by which we were supposed to operate went out the window. And not only was I in love with a beautiful redhead who adored me, but she was more than likely pregnant with my kid! What if Ida had conceived tonight? The more I thought about it, as I took the short drive to the Vine Street house, the more I felt like a sheik out of the Arabian Nights, the caliph with that marvelous harem and dozens of kids from different mothers floating around all over the place. How did *that* scenario fit into wartime America with its Victorian and Puritan measuring stick? Maybe that's why I liked the seedy jazz joints late at night. There was no pretense there. Just the simple, primal, honest instincts of people from all walks of life seeking the simplicity of a golden nugget hidden in an F-chord or a whiskey sour. But I couldn't think about those things this evening.

The Unexpected Highway

In the morning, the four of us picked up State Route 99 downtown and sped toward Fresno. When I had gotten in and kissed Eleanor the night before, I somehow felt she might have smelled another woman on me. Even a shower can't cover up the lingering odors that seep out of the pores...maybe even for days to come. But if she did, Eleanor said nothing. Maybe I didn't feel guilty about Ida, so what? I'd known that little gal a lot longer than I'd known Eleanor. In some men, a fear that one woman isn't going to be security enough haunts them, so they keep another hanging around somewhere on a shelf just in case he might need her. Was I doing that unconsciously? My gut told me Ida would be thinking about me until she saw the red of my bloodshot eyes again. She would build herself up, now that her womanhood was fully awake, and desire would rear its restless head. Then she'd have to have it over and over again, until sex became a regular part of her life and she found that she didn't want to live without it. Well, at least that was the picture I painted from my well of experience. If she was carrying a child, then heaven help the guy who wants just a lover. Motherhood changes a woman's hormones and "Dad" gets relegated to bringing in the bacon and mowing the lawn.

"Ya know, this is the first vacation I've ever taken," Boots was saying as we sped along.

"Not me," Fred spoke up. "We went all the time. Canada, France, Italy, Greece, Spain, England...and even some of the U.S. National Parks. I got sick of traveling. I just wanted to stay home by the pool and bake in the sun."

Eleanor laughed. "And me, I couldn't wait to hit the road. I would've stayed months in those places if Mom and Dad had let me. I felt like a sponge, soaking up everything I could about a culture...a way of life that was different from my own. What about you, Cable? Are you a traveler?"

"Well, not really by choice...but my pursuits have taken me to some of those places...or sometimes it was because someone was in pursuit of me.", I laughed. "But mostly cops are like fixtures. They hang around the same beats and haunts until they grow old. Then when it's too late, they take a good long look and chalk up what they think they might've missed."

"And what have you missed?" Fred inquired, leaning forward from the back seat to put her hands on the cushion.

I patted Eleanor's hand. "It's right here. Sometimes we don't even know what we want. But I'm happy to report I recognized it before it was too late."

Eleanor grabbed my right arm with both of her hands and hung on to it. She laid her head on my shoulder and closed her eyes. "It's all like a miracle. Every bit of it. That two people—"

"—Before you two get too dreamy, there was a sign back there that said the Yosemite turn off was five miles ahead," Boots muttered.

We turned off and drove for another ninety minutes or so. Finally we were at the entrance to Yosemite Valley. As we descended, the landscape changed into the kind of splendor you only see on postcards in L.A. Suddenly a huge valley opened up with granite peaks on both sides. Half-Dome shone in the afternoon light and deer grazed by the banks of the Merced River. I thought no place on earth could ever excel this. And now my life seemed to be settling. Next to me was a woman I felt I could hunker down with the rest of my days.

When we got into the Awahnee, I called Al Newley up at Glacier Point. They had just put in a phone line recently and his voice was clear and present. "Cable, glad you guys made it. Now, I've arranged for the four of you to stay up here tonight after the display. Just tell Sy at the desk to reserve your room there for tomorrow night. I assume you want your fiancée to see the falls and all, eh?'

"Yeah, Al, that's swell. So how do we get to you?"

"You hike the four miles up from the trail head at the bottom of Glacier point. Just bring your toothbrush. We got the rest up here." I thanked Al, hung up and told the others the plan.

"I'm afeared those hikin' days are over for me," Boots complained. "I'll stay here with binoculars, if ya don't mind."

We all agreed to let Boots have the room at the Ah-wahnee. After a short rest and a couple of drinks, we started for the trail head. It was a hell of a climb up that mountainside. I was outta shape, but the girls zipped right up. What seemed like hours later we reached the plateau where we found Al Newley and the large chalet-style Glacier Point Hotel near the falls.

He greeted us in his tough guy, warm voice. "Damn, if it isn't the night crawler from L.A.!" he barked. We embraced. "Damn, not one but *two* gorgeous babes! How do you rate, Cable? By chance, is one of you available to be *my* date for a drink after my duties?"

"Sure, sailor, I'm all yours." Fred laughed. "Those two...well, they probably will want to be left alone. Almost honeymooners, you know."

I introduced everyone and we sat for about an hour laughing and having a good ol' time. We drank a little, talked a lot. We had noticed a group of young men attending a huge pile of burning, smoking bark. "It's Red Fir bark," Al Newley said. "We only get it from dead or downed trees. It's better fuel than wood. We get red hot coals out of this pile...and at precisely 9:00 p.m., we push it evenly over the falls there," he pointed to the granite spillway. "Three thousand, one hundred feet to the bottom, folks."

As it got dark, Fred decided to stick around Al and watch. Eleanor took my hand and a shiver went through her. When the sun went down this high up, a cold chill fell upon the mountaintop, even in summertime. "How close to the edge can we go?" she asked me.

"You know, that's what Henry David Thoreau said...'I walk along the sea, as close to the water's edge as I dare go,' or something like that," I said. "Let's see how far *we* can go."

We walked away from the other people preparing the Fire Falls. Far in the west remained the faintest glow of the dying sun. "Oh, Cable. I wish I could have you like this forever. I've never seen you so relaxed. If this was the last day of my life, I would want it to be just like this."

I took that woman in my arms and kissed her with everything I had. In that moment I suddenly realized how mature this love was. She clung to me, kissing every part of my face. "Tonight, Cable, I want you to fill me again and again with you, until I am dizzy from it!"

I grabbed her hand and we walked on, closer and closer to the three-thousand foot precipice. We held to each other tightly as we leaned over. But we couldn't see all the way down. There was a small rise above us. We walked up there and this time we could see the campfires of the tourists below, little yellow lights in the darkening night.

Suddenly a chill caught me. It was as if my intuition were up and doing flips. Some dark shadow had entered into our company. I spun around to see—and there was what I couldn't have imagined in a hundred years. Krieger stood alone with a gun pointed right at us. Eleanor shrieked as I tried to compose myself. "Krieger, you're worse than that proverbial bad penny. How in the hell did you find us?"

"Your old...sidekick, Mr. Blake. He wasn't very cooperative when I ground out a cigarette on his forehead, but when threatened with a burning cigarette in his eye, he...uh...how do you say?...sang like a bird.

"You cruel and worthless son-of-a-bitch! I oughta plug ya now...did you kill him, too?"

"Oh Mr. Denning, you misjudge me. I never kill someone who might be useful later. And what if he had lied to me? We would have had to have another conversation. Relax, Mr. Denning, I left him in the hotel tied to a nice comfy chair."

"Throw your weapon over to me, Mr. Denning," he said changing his tone. "Come...out of your pocket...on the ground."

"I don't think so, Krieger. There are too many people. You'll be seen before you can finish—"

"—You might wish that. But alas, it is five minutes to nine. They will be too busy to notice and it will be too noisy to hear the gun shots."

"Come an' get me, Krieger...leave Eleanor out of it."

"You Americans are so stupid, Denning. Is not there an old popular song, *You Always Kill the One You Love*—appropriate, don't you think?" He laughed.

"The Mills Brothers, Krieger, and it's 'You Always *Hurt* the One You Love,' you dumb shit! Plus the gun in my pocket is pointed at your head!"

"Same thing, in a way. I know it's dark up here, but you must believe me. *My* gun is going back and forth, trying to decide which one of you I shall kill first. I believe in your old west, was this not called a...uh.. *stand-off*?"

Al Newley was directing the hot coals from the Red Fir piles faster now. We could no longer see the dozens of tourists gathered at the bottom of the 3,000 ft. drop because we had slowly moved away from the precipice. But I could hear a man from below call out "Hello Glacier Point." There was an exchange of calls that ended with "Let the fire fall" then "The fire falls!" Then we could hear the cheers begin as the stream of coals started to slide over the falls and splash into the waters below. "Try and get *me*, Krieger, c'mon, let the dame walk. Get *me*, you cowardly bastard. You don't know how anxious I am to spill your brains over this waterfall!"

"Cable! No! Darling, please!" Eleanor shrieked.

"I've always liked your anger, Mr. Denning. When you're this 'hopped up', as you Americans say, *murder becomes you*." He looked closer to the edge of the precipice. "Oh, dear, did I tell you I have a fear of heights?" He waived his gun again, back and forth between Eleanor and me. "Hmm...which one? Husband-to-be? Wife-to-be? Oh, and I've heard...*baby* to be! A family portrait, right before me. Touching. Soon there will be too many people in the world. We have a plan. The *Lichter Grabstätte* intends world domination by somewhere around the second decade of the twenty-first century. America will have a short glory...just as you and your expecting wife-to-be, a very short...almost honeymoon, Mr. Denning."

I had fooled him before...I thought I could fool him again. I had to distract him. Eleanor was shaking and I shoved her away from me, hoping Krieger wouldn't see that well in the dark. "Why did you kill Maya Stoldthedder and Zorrie Robles, Krieger...or should I say, *Zimmer-Kleiber*?"

"Ahhh...so, Maya told you about that, did she. Well, perhaps they were for...uh...shall I say, target practice? After a while, it gets easier and easier...eh Mr. Denning?"

I guessed right. His night vision wasn't as good as mine. Eleanor trembled about twelve feet from me now. "You creep! You worthless piece of shit! It's because of the likes of you that I'm out there in the trenches, scraping up the other scum and vermin like you that fuck up people's lives!"

"Very poetic, Mr. Denning. But either way, one of you is dead. I hope both, but we cannot always have things just the way we'd like them now, can we?"

I knew none of us could wait any longer. There was a small but thick branch in front of me about two feet. I lunged for the piece of wood and tossed it at Krieger with all of my strength. Three shots rang out. Then three more. The fire falls workers nearby started yelling to each other and scattered. Now Krieger and I each had three shots left. The branch had missed him but I could see him on his knees. He dropped on one knee. I must have hit him. Eleanor came running toward me...

"Eleanor, no!!" I shouted. But as she approached me Krieger emptied his last three shots into her and then fell forward, dead.

Eleanor screamed and collapsed into my arms, mortally wounded. I cried out with such ferocity to the sky that the people who had been running, stopped and turned to run over to assist.

As Eleanor's life-blood gushed and ebbed from her beautiful body, I lost all sense of reason. Suddenly I was disconnected from the earth and everything that ever had to do with it. I pounded the ground, rocked her into my bosom, and whimpered like a wounded child of the universe. "Somebody—all of you—anybody—help me, please help me get this lady to a hospital!"

Al Newley rushed over and assessed the situation. "Oh, God! It would take hours to carry her down the mountain and then we'd have to call Fresno for an ambulance, Cable! I'm sorry...so sorry!"

"Do *something*...I beg you!"

Several well-meaning men formed around Eleanor's body to pick it up. But I knew it was too late. She was dead. One of Krieger's last bullets had penetrated her heart, the second went through her neck, severing the jugular vein. I fell across the men to stop them. I made them go away with motions of my arms and soon there was just Eleanor and me...holding her in my arms...and the cold night winds of the Sierra Nevada. Now we could float away together into the night sky. Nobody would notice.

Epilogue

When a man goes insane I'm not sure he knows it. But I think I was insane for a few weeks. Thanks to Boots and his loving 'tough-talk' I was able to return to my office by September, 1942. Fred had paid my rent from Eleanor's estate. Faithful Ida had maintained my office, took the phone calls, answered the mail and kept the place clean enough for me to return home to clean sheets and a swept floor. Home, did I say? Eleanor had become my home. We buried her at Forest Lawn, ironically not too far from Michelangelo's David, right along side Zorrie Robles. Eleanor would have wanted that.

What I was afraid would happen... had happened. Once again the vile and depraved elements of my work had violently ripped away my chance for love. Once again... the beautiful, innocent woman who was ready and willing to settle for whatever I could give of myself, would die a premature death—and I would survive. For what—?

Now I would return to the vagabond private eye I really was, a street gypsy with a legal license to track down errant husbands and wives, lovers, boyfriends, girlfriends...and who knows what else lurked out there in the dark streets of this city....its underbelly pulsating with dirty little secrets.

Fred and Boots brought me up to my office the day I returned. I looked around. I could see Ida's handiwork. "You know, Cable, you don't have to do this. Eleanor told me that all she owned was yours....before...well, you know. So you don't have to work."

I gave Fred a half-smile. "You're okay, kid. But ya know? I'm made of the same cloth as Boots here. We wouldn't know what to do with all that dough. You take my share, Fred. We've all suffered through this. And I'll tell ya what. Let's all remain friends, and if Boots or I ever need a hand-out, we'll call on you."

Fred hugged and kissed both of us. As she held me, she stepped back slightly and said softly. "Cable, you know we love you. And like in that motion picture we saw together, if you ever need me, just whistle..." She smiled and left.

Boots slapped me across the shoulder. "Well, you ol' son-of-a-bitch. Now ya gotta pull the whole lot of it back together. Make it work, Cable. Ya know how much I lament Eleanor's passin', simple ol' shit that I am. But through all the bullshit and tragedy, I hope ya learned your lesson. This world ain't what it used to be when I was the law, son. The lines aren't clear anymore and they're all gray and fuzzed up. Stick to the Kodak pictures. Ya won't get rich, but it's a damn sight safer. Ain't that better?"

Was it? I didn't know. Boots hadn't recovered well from his encounter with Krieger and his feelings of guilt about giving up our location. After Krieger left him tied to the chair, Boots had smashed the chair repeatedly against the wall until it was on the floor in pieces. He tried to get help to us, but it was too late. I hugged Boots good-bye and looked out my window as the last of the old cowboy sheriffs limped away, his pride hurt and his shoulders slumping from life's burdens. Yeah, that's how I'd probably end up. Just keep snapping pictures, argue with irate husbands over their wives' infidelity, and like an aging animal, walk my territory until I was old and gray and slouched—and I could wear a worn-out cardigan sweater and sit on park benches, coughing and spitting up the remnants of my life. Yeah, ya know, Boots was a good teacher.

I started for my bedroom. "Welcome back, Mr. Denning," a pleasant young voice spoke. "Uh, I didn't want to disturb you..."

Poking her head around the doorway stood Ida Latney. "Ida! Thanks for everything, kid. Ya treated the old ship well and kept the decks clean while I was gone. But ya gotta remember rule number one: when we're just the two of us, it's *Cable*, comprendo?"

She ran to me, checked my eyes to see if it was okay. I smiled and she fell into my arms holding me like a clam closing up for the night. "Cable! I thought every horrible thought there was to think in the world! I cried for your loss. I am so terribly, terribly sorry. And you don't ever have to tell me, I know... you really loved her."

It was hard to believe this young woman had the layers of understanding and sensitivity she did. But you know, she *did*. I put my head in my hands as she pulled away. "Yeah. I don't know where I am, or where I'm goin' any more, Ida. And that's my truth—at least today." I looked at her stomach. It was still flat. "Am I...uh, am I to assume that you're not..."

"No, I'm not," she said sadly. "*My truth*...is that I wanted to be.... I told you I would never regret it."

I came up to her and kissed her on the forehead. "Ya know, Ida, like in some crazy movie I just saw, 'this could be the beginning of a beautiful friendship'."

229

She grabbed her purse and started for the door. "If you need anything, please call. When do you want me to come in again? There are a lot of phone calls to make and letters to answer—I mean, when you feel up to it."

"Well, how about tomorrow? And every day five days a week until we can't stand each other anymore?"

The young woman beamed from ear to ear. "Yes, Mr..... ah, Cable...I'll be by in the morning."

"Not too early, Ida...you know these older men..."

I didn't know if I could ever go to the Hollywood Dam again. But one day, months later, I did. There I was, standing at the railing looking across the water towards the end of the day, much like Eleanor and I had done together. Trying to imagine her there....yeah, sometimes I could feel her. My memory of her frozen in time....she would always be young and beautiful. I even thought of that wise little alien, Kylell, floating up there somewhere in the cosmos, rejoined with his own kind....and strangely that made me smile.

But today was Eleanor's. "I'm here, babe, remember?" I said out loud. I was recalling what I told her that evening we stood here unable not to touch each other.... *if you're lucky enough for 'it' to come along, you won't know what to do with it.* Because of her, maybe I would know what to do with it now. I smiled as a breeze rose up from the lake and the smell of sage filled my nostrils. I could hear Eleanor's voice echoing across the water— words from her note I had memorized.

It is my prayer, Cable, that in some beautiful moment your heart will burst open enough for you to know how much you are loved. For if one keeps passing by when true love is offered, then it could be lost forever. My darling, this is only the first page of my love song to you. Come home when you can....

Suddenly, a new music wafted through the air of my heart; and I knew that this earth as it existed could never be good enough for this kind of love. I knew that I would go on talking in some strange man's voice, going through the motions that posed as living—just as I had done before. Yeah....another piece of me had died three thousand feet above Yosemite Valley. But I would keep going for a while. Maybe if we chisel out little pieces of goodness here and there, we might make a difference. I don't know. People stink. What's wrong with us, anyway? Maybe it was like little Kylell said. We are forever space travelers, looking for our points of origin, not quite fulfilled here on earth, but gazing up at the sky on a starry night, longing to go home. Yeah, that sounded pretty good. I would go home one day.

Home...where love is...

The End

Acknowledgements

Cover images:
Background - Yosemite Firefalls — Ralph Crane Artworks

Peg O' My Heart image — Art Frahm 1940's illustration
    By permission from his daughter, Diana Armstrong
Cable Denning image — Kenneth R. Cox - photographer
Blonde model image — © deanpowell.com - photographer
Asian model image —Crystal Cartier photography
Silhouette gunman — © CanStock Photo, Inc./Ostill

Original Cover Designs: Frances Walker-Moss

Editing and Research Consultant: Frances Walker-Moss

www.ingramcontent.com/pod-product-compliance
Lightning Source LLC
Chambersburg PA
CBHW020653030726
47498CB00002B/487